# TORMENTED

# FROM THE EDGE

# BOOK SIX

# BY EVIE RILEY

TORMENTED

FROM THE EDGE

BOOK SIX


COPYRIGHT © 2022

EVIE RILEY

SECOND EDITION

ISBN: 978-1-77357-697-8

PUBLISHED BY NAUGHTY NIGHTS PRESS LLC

COVER ART BY WILLSIN ROWE

# TORMENTED

**He will fight for their future...**

Sol and his little brother escaped the abuse of their foster father only to end up on the streets. Always on the move, they wind up in a small town that oddly feels like home. It's the first place that ever has, so they make plans to stick around and set up in a local tent city.

Sol keeps River safe and healthy no matter what, but after their home is raided, Sol is worried about their future. River's new social worker offers help that Sol just can't refuse. Despite his growing attraction to Isaiah, Sol is convinced the older man could never want someone as tainted and broken as he is.

Isaiah sees beyond to the caring big

brother who has given everything to make sure his sibling is provided for. The social worker doesn't care about Sol's past. Despite the fact the two brothers have been homeless for the last four years, it doesn't define either of them.

Nor does it change the way Isaiah views the man Sol has become. Truth is, he finds Sol simply amazing and his attraction to the younger man is undeniable. The two are caught up in an emotional upheaval one night when River goes missing. As he comforts Sol, Isaiah realizes he can no longer keep his feelings to himself.

Can the two forge the kind of future together that Sol has never dreamed possible?

# CHAPTER ONE

Isaiah

I LET OUT a sigh as I looked at the mess of paperwork that was currently spread all across my dining room table. I knew when I accepted the position that working for the task force I was going to have a great deal of work ahead of me. However, I knew it would be worth it to help children in need. I just never expected for it to be this hard, for it to hit this close to home.

The task force had been working with the local authorities just five hundred miles from town. They were made aware of a Fundamentalist Church of Jesus Christ of Latter-Day Saints, FLDS, stronghold where they sent children they deemed were in need of repenting. The compound was heavily guarded with FLDS security that used military grade weapons. We still weren't sure how they got a hold of the regulated weapons. The team was trying to look into it and track down how they received the weapons.

Like all takedown operations that involved children, I went with the team to the FLDS stronghold. I stayed back in the van until the area had been cleared and secured. For most, it wouldn't have been a big deal to go into the stronghold and see the children. However, for me, I knew exactly what to expect within the compound.

I had been one of the unfortunate children born into the FLDS. My mother was my father's eighteenth wife and she was only twelve when they got married. The Prophet had told my father that he needed more wives to produce more children for him to be allowed to enter the Golden Kingdom when he died. The problem was, there were only so many women old enough to legally be married.

Not that they really got married.

Anyone after the first wife was purely a spiritual wife. Still, the amount of single females over the age of eighteen dwindled down drastically over the years. My mother was fourteen when she gave birth to me and I am one of twenty-eight siblings.

For the first eighteen years of my life, I dealt with being abused and neglected by my father and my mother. My father, I would only see him once or twice a year. He was always too busy with his other wives or working to truly pay any attention to us. My mother was too broken by my father to take care of us. She had ten children, nine after me, and by that point she had lost all traces of her own identity. She spent her days looking out the window, waiting for when my father would walk up the path.

With my mother being checked out, everything rested on my shoulders.

We all lived in homes that should have been condemned. There was no running water, no electricity, and there were only three bedrooms, leaving five kids in a room. The rooms weren't even big enough for proper beds. We all slept together on the floor, on a king size mattress.

There was no such thing as personal space.

There was no such thing as privacy.

The single bathroom in the house barely worked and we often had to go out into the woods to use the bathroom. We rarely got to shower and get clean. We used to have to use rain barrels and hope we would have enough water to get clean once a week.

The place was always dirty, despite the amount of hours I would spend cleaning it. We had cockroaches and mice running all over the place. You would be sleeping and get bitten by something and have no idea what it was.

The food we would get was always just

about rotten or already rotten. It was all we could afford with the very miniscule amount of money that we got from my father. It was up to me to cook and as I got older, I got more creative with the food. I had been able to come up with different meals to make with the same food. My siblings appreciated it, and it made me feel good to see the pleasure on their faces at the delicious taste.

It was then that I discovered my love of cooking. I loved knowing that I could make someone happy by just eating my food. It encouraged me to try different things and to see what else I could come up with and my siblings never said no to trying something I cooked.

Within the FLDS, children were home schooled or taught by the church and it was never anything that would be recognized by the State as proper schooling.

I would sneak out and learn down at the community center. I had to be careful and keep it hidden, because if I had been caught I would have been sent to the reform camp to repent for my sins, leaving my siblings to fend for themselves.

Problems had come up over the years before I turned eighteen. The most common was my father pressuring me to find a wife, or my father trying to set one of my younger sisters up with a husband.

When I turned eighteen, I had my escape plan ready.

No one could just leave the FLDS. They ruled with intimidation and abuse. I had already experienced it enough from my father and my uncles over the eighteen years of being trapped there.

I had tried to get all of my siblings to leave with me, but I could only get five of them to agree to leave. I was okay with that, though, because the five that I did get were my sisters. They were my full blooded sisters and despite not being able to get my half-sisters, I knew that getting five of them out with me was more than I could have hoped for. They were all underage and that made it very difficult and, technically, I committed five counts of kidnapping that I could still be charged with to this day should it ever get out.

Still, I had never regretted it for a single second.

That night, I'd had everything planned.

We had all packed a bag so we were ready. My sisters all shared a room so I didn't have to worry about anyone spotting them leaving. With me being eighteen, I was free to leave the house should I wish.

I had said goodbye to my brothers and got the girls out through their bedroom window. We had to walk through the dark ten miles to a car that was waiting for us.

I had reached out to a woman that helped FLDS members to escape the cult. She knew to be prepared for six of us, but I had neglected to inform her of my sisters' ages. She wasn't happy, but she was not about to turn them away. She knew all too well what fate awaited them back at the compound.

We drove out of state into Nevada, adding more charges against me, until we arrived at my aunt's home. She had gotten out when she was twenty and had space for us to hide out. Once we arrived, my aunt was already set to take all of us in.

Our saving grace was that Nevada was a safe haven state. Even if the police caught us, they would never send my siblings back to my parents. We would be able to get sanctuary for them and that was all that I cared about.

I had only stayed for two months in the summer before I was off to College. I wanted to get my Masters in Social Work so I would be able to help save more children like my siblings. Now, fifteen years later, my sisters were still living their lives free from the FLDS, and I worked for a Federal Task Force helping to stop crimes against children.

The loud trill of my phone ringing pulled me out of my reminiscing thoughts and I glanced at the screen, noting it was Travis Manning calling. Travis was another social worker helping with the task force and we had become very good friends.

I had been worried about Travis recently, though, because he'd been acting differently. I had seen a couple of bruises on him, too, but he had dismissed them as it being a result of a self-defense class.

I could tell he wasn't telling me the full truth, right away.

Travis had a tell when he was lying, he always looked away slightly. He was such a good man that he couldn't look someone in the eye and lie to them. I knew that I couldn't help him until he was ready to ask for help. I just hoped that whatever was going on, it was something that he could survive.

"Hey, Travis, you working late, too?" I

asked as I answered the phone.

"The one hundred and five case files currently sitting on my floor have decided sleep is for the weak," he joked lightly.

"I know. When I agreed to being on the task force as a social worker, I didn't expect to have this much paperwork. Nor this many cases of children I needed to place. We're running out of foster homes."

That was my biggest concern.

The task force had federal clearance so they could go all over the country to work any cases and chase after any criminal. It was great because it allowed them to get the worst criminals against children off the streets and either in jail or in the ground.

The problem was, though, the children that were left behind after these cases. Some could be placed in foster homes locally, but there were also children that needed a place to go until we could find their family. We had a lot of children stuck in a transition position because we were trying to track down a next of kin for them.

Or they were seventeen and only had months left. We didn't want a bunch of newly eighteen years olds being homeless on the streets, so we were trying to find a place for them to go.

In town, we had a motel that gave us a weekly voucher for the homeless or newly aged out foster kids that needed a place to stay for a week or so until they could get on their feet. However, it wasn't enough for the kids that needed more than a week. We had to find another solution and that also rested on our shoulders.

"I know, that is why I have spoken with Dominic O'Conner. He is new in town and has purchased the Capitol building. That's where Eli is currently living. Dom has expressed interest in helping the children. He had a good size settlement from the death of his son and has been investing it to generate more capital. I thought I could set up a meeting between the two of you and maybe you could come up with some sort of longer term solution."

If we had even one person who would invest in helping financially with a new group home of sorts, that could help. We would need to find other investors for it to be sustainable, but if we had the connection of getting started with Dominic, that could be what we need to get a group home up and running.

"Okay, set it up and I'll see what I can do."

"I'll reach out to him tomorrow. We gotta do something before the foster homes get too many children and we risk them being neglected or abused."

"No, I agree, something has to give before the system breaks more than it already is. We are finally getting the system back together, I don't want it to slip and go back to how it used to be."

"We'll get it worked out. Now, tell me, what are you eating?" Travis asked, and I could hear the smile in his voice.

Everyone knew I liked food. That was not that surprising considering I was above average in terms of body weight. I wasn't overweight, but I did have a Dad Bod.

After growing up barely being able to

eat, when I turned eighteen and had money for proper food, I tended to eat quite a bit. At first, I burned through it easily enough, but as I got older my metabolism slowed down and it got harder for me to lose the weight.

Cooking had also become something that brought me comfort and stress relief. Whenever I was feeling stressed or upset, I would cook something. It helped to calm me down and it made me feel better. Dr. Holland, the psychologist at work, had informed me that it wasn't the worst coping mechanism out there. I wasn't drinking or doing drugs to relieve the stress. I knew what he wasn't saying, though. Eventually, I would be putting my health at risk, all the same. If I gained too much weight, I was looking at high blood pressure, diabetes, and high cholesterol.

None of which would be good and could do the same damage that drinking or drugs would do to my body. I knew I needed to try and find a way to lose some weight or to cook less, but I didn't have the drive for that, currently.

"Just some leftover chicken alfredo pasta that I made before we had to head out. It's nothing fancy, but I had a new recipe to cook it in a slow cooker."

"Sounds good. How is it?"

"It's good. Anything I can make in a slow cooker, I am happy to try."

"Same, I have to get a new slow cooker because I have used mine so much it's dead now."

I could understand that all too well. With our jobs, it is rarely nine to five and we are often stuck at the office working late. A slow cooker allowed us to work any number of hours and come home to a freshly cooked meal. It was a huge saving grace in my life and I was always looking for unique recipes for it.

"I just got a new one on sale before we got hit with this case. It was only thirty bucks and it holds enough for six people," I supplied.

"Shit, I gotta get me one. I'll go out and grab it tomorrow. I don't need to eat that much, but I like to make a huge batch and freeze it."

"Absolutely. I do that all the time. It makes life so much easier," I easily agreed.

"I'll let you go so you can get back to work. Or we both can, I should say. I'll see you tomorrow."

"Always. Good night, Travis."

"Goodnight."

I ended the call and placed my phone back down on the table. I let out a sigh as I looked at all of the case folders that were covering my table. I had a long night ahead of me, but I knew I would never make it through all of this work in one night. I would stay up for a couple more hours before I headed off to bed to get six hours of sleep. Tomorrow, I would get back to finding these children safe homes and, hopefully, they would no longer have to live in fear.

# CHAPTER TWO

Sol

"WHEN DO YOU have to leave?" River asked me.

"I need to head out in a few minutes, Bear," I answered as I finished brushing my hair.

We had been in town for a week, now, and I still wasn't too certain how long we would stay here. We were currently living in the tent city that the town had. My little brother, River, who was twelve—I still couldn't believe he was twelve already—was very good with moving. We had been doing this for four years, now.

I hated that we were homeless, that my little brother had to grow up living outside and not having a proper room for himself. The trick was, I didn't know what else to do for him.

Our parents were both Native American, but they were not in love with each other. Our father was often in and out of jail and when he was out, he wasn't around. Our mother tended to spend all of her money on booze and it left us with nothing. When I was eleven, we were both taken away from her and put into the foster system.

At the time, we were placed with a

single male, Phillip Morris, and we were his only foster children. It was like a dream come true to us. We both got to have our own room, there was always food in the fridge, there was heat when it got cold, and we even had air conditioning.

Phillip had been really nice and always helped us with our homework, made us lunches for school, and cooked us dinner. We had chores, but we were good with it. It all seemed like a dream for us.

That dream only lasted a month though, for me.

One month until the first time Phillip came into my bedroom in the middle of the night and started to touch me. I didn't know what was happening, at first, and he had told me it was our special time together, that it was a secret and I couldn't tell anyone. He even threatened to hurt River if I said anything. That always made me stay quiet, even when it went from touching to rape.

It continued on for four years, until I was fifteen. Over the previous four years, Phillip still treated us well, especially River. He still made sure we had food, and he always made sure we had clothes for school and money for any field trips. On the outside, he looked like the perfect foster father to the both of us.

However, at night, he was in my room doing horrible things to me.

Things no grown ass man should be doing to a child.

When I turned fifteen, I could tell I was getting too old for him. He stopped doing those small touches to me during the day, and instead he had been turning his interest and attention toward River. I knew I had to get us out of there before Phillip started to molest my little brother. It was my job to protect him and I was not about to allow River to go through anything that I'd had to go through. It was perfectly fine for me to be broken, but I would be damned if I allowed River to be broken, too.

I had packed our bags and hid them under my bed. After Phillip left me alone that night, I went into River's bedroom and got him ready. We snuck out his bedroom window and headed off into the night.

At the time, River was only eight and didn't understand why we had to leave. To him, we had a good life, and I couldn't blame him. It was a good life, if I ignored the sexual abuse I experienced every night.

If I could have guarantees that Phillip would never touch River, I would have stayed for the next three years. I would have waited to take River with me until I was eighteen and legally an adult. However, I knew Phillip would target River and I was not going to allow anything like that to happen to him. River was innocent and I was damned determined to keep it that way.

He had whined and complained in the beginning, but as the months passed he did get over it and accepted that this was our life. We traveled on freight trains as stowaways all the time.

There were other homeless people who just rode the trains all over the country. They had given me some pointers that had helped me get used to living on the street. I had learned that you never spend more than six months at a time in a city. The shorter the duration you were there, the better your odds were of not getting caught.

However, if you stayed too little time, you risked not having enough money to survive in the next town. I found that six months was the sweet spot. It kept us safe from the police finding us and it allowed me to have enough money saved up from the odd jobs I took to keep us going in the next town until I could find yet another a cash job.

I had been able to save up and get us a tent that we used in the tent cities at every new location. River had been amazing with all of the travels. It helped that he loved learning about different people's stories in each new city.

River was smart. I suspected he was a genius, but I had no way of knowing for certain. He wasn't able to go to school with us being homeless. Not to mention, we both had to be listed as a missing person. I was nineteen, now, but that didn't change that I could be up on kidnapping charges if the police ever got a hold of me. I did technically transport River across multiple state lines during the past four years. I wasn't sure how it would all work out with us being siblings, but it wasn't worth the risk to try to put him into a school. Not to mention us moving every six months would send up multiple red flags in the system.

Whenever I had to work, I left River with someone within the tent city. Soon, with him getting older, I wouldn't have to do that. I could technically leave him alone now at the age of twelve, but it made me feel better knowing someone was watching him. I did have to give them half of my pay from that day, but even fifty percent of my pay was better than not making anything that day.

River truly did enjoy it, too. He loved learning all about the different people and hearing their own unique stories. He had a deep love for learning and he would take whatever he could get.

"Who is going to watch me?" River asked.

"Max said he would keep an eye on you while I go and see if I can get a job."

Max was one of the younger guys here in the tent city. He also wasn't going to charge me anything to watch River, something I appreciated greatly. I wasn't sure how long he had been here or why he was homeless. That wasn't something anybody talked about. I was just appreciative of Max being willing to watch River for me.

River also liked him.

Max was smart, too. He seemed too smart to be homeless, but you never know what is going on with a person inside of their mind. Max could easily have a mental illness that made it difficult for him to hold down a job. He could have been a veteran, for all I knew. I learned long ago to stop judging people based on their life and appearances. Anything could make someone homeless and I wouldn't want to be judged myself over it.

"Yes! He is so cool. And he knows some pretty impressive math," River said, flashing a big smile.

"He seems like a nice man. Best

behavior for him," I said, but I knew that River was always well behaved. He was *too* well behaved, in my opinion.

Kids needed to be able to make messes and get into some trouble. River was always so well behaved you would think he was an adult. There had been plenty of times when I had to force him to be a kid and play some games and have fun.

I hated that he didn't truly know the joy of having friends, but at the same time, he didn't seem like the type of kid that wanted to have friends his age. He was too smart for his own good and it affected him socially. He needed help, but I had no idea what to do for him other than try and socialize him with kids his own age.

We would go to the public library and he would hang out there, but he spent most of the time reading book after book instead of talking with the other kids. I was hoping, eventually, we would find a town that we both wanted to stay in and I could try and make a real life for him. He was twelve. He was reaching the age of needing to have his own life and a stable home. I didn't want him to be homeless and living in tent cities when he was a teenager. It would become far too dangerous for him, then.

"Always," River said, as he rolled his eyes.

"All right, let's go. I have that meeting so, hopefully, I can get a job and we can have some food again," I said as I guided River out of the tent.

We hadn't really eaten anything major in the past couple of days. We'd only had a few snacks here and there. Last night,

Max had given River a can of soup, which I appreciated immensely. The more people I had looking out for River, the better off he would be.

After waving to Max as River ran over to him, I made my way down a few miles down the highway to the nearest construction site. I had found that working in construction sites gave me the highest chances of a cash job.

A lot of construction foremen would hire migrant workers and pay them cash each day. They got to save money and they didn't have to worry about insurance or paying taxes on that worker. I had no problem with it, because it meant cash each day and it would allow me to have skills that could transfer to any city we were in.

I also enjoyed the work. I liked working

with my hands and it was nice to be able to work out and stay in shape. I would often go to the gym when I was younger and work out. I played a lot of sports and enjoyed being active. Working in construction was a free gym to me.

Finding the construction site was easy enough. With a town on the smaller side, there weren't many construction projects going on. It was also easy to walk from one end to the other and all I had to do was go in the direction of the tall construction crane. I had never used one, personally, but I had always wanted to.

I did love working in construction and I would have loved to get my certificates to operate heavy machinery construction equipment. That would require us to stay in a town long enough for me to save up the money to take the courses, and so far, that didn't happen in six months.

Maybe one day, though.

I was only nineteen.

I had a lot of years left in me.

The second I arrived at the construction site, I was impressed by the sheer size of it. I had been expecting for it to be homes or an apartment building, but this site was three times the size of any apartment construction site I had been on previously.

I made my way over to the main trailer where I knew the foreman or the owner would be. I knocked on the door and after a moment it opened to reveal a younger looking man. I had been expecting to find a forty something year old man easily, not one in his twenties.

"Hello, Sir, my name is Sol. I am looking for work," I said.

I never told anyone that my full name was Solomon. One, it normally got some weird looks, and two, if they knew my full first name it would be easier for someone to find us. There weren't that many Solomon within the missing person's database. It was one more precaution that I took.

"Hey, I'm Zane. Come on in," he said, flashing me a warm smile as he stepped back.

I headed inside the trailer and, to my surprise, he went around to stand behind the desk. He was the actual owner and that brought up more questions. He must have come from a wealthy family to be running a construction site like this. Or maybe it belonged to his parents and it was passed down to him.

"I've worked in construction for four

years now, Sir," I started, but stopped when Zane waved his hand at me.

"It's Zane. You don't have to call me Sir. You have a kid brother, right?" he asked and instantly my defenses skyrocketed.

There shouldn't be any reason for him to think I had a little brother. If he had someone watching us, we would need to leave right away.

"Whoa, relax. No one is spying on you. The town is growing but we are still small at heart. And when someone new is spotted around town, people get interested. My soon-to-be brother in-law, Devon, is a cop. He used to be homeless, and ever since he graduated the academy, he likes to keep an eye on the homeless communities to make sure they are doing okay. He saw you and your brother. He figured you might be coming to me to look for work. He said you looked like a construction guy. Can't say I disagree."

I wasn't sure how I felt about that. I didn't like people knowing that I had a little brother. It wasn't that I was ashamed of River or wanted to keep him hidden away, I just knew it was safer for people to not know about him.

I didn't look like I was in my late twenties or early thirties. I looked like a nineteen year old and River looked like a twelve year old boy. I couldn't be put into the foster system, but he still could be and if someone knew he was homeless, someone could call child protective services on me and I could lose him. It's why we had to be so careful to ensure he would get to stay with me and not be potentially abused in one of the homes.

"He's very well taken care of," I said in my defense. It wasn't like I could run from here. That would just cause more suspicion.

"I'm not saying he isn't. Nor is Devon. Like I said, Devon used to be homeless. He ran away from home when he was a young teenager when his father almost killed him. He knows bad things happen. His best friend had to deal with being abused in the foster system before he became homeless after aging out. Now, both are engaged to the love of their lives and have a stable home and career. Devon likes to pay it forward and so do I. There's no judgment on our parts. I am happy to take you on as a worker. I would love to offer you an official job, but I know you won't take it just yet."

He was right. I couldn't take the

offered official job just yet. It wasn't that I didn't want to. I would have loved to make more than the cash I would be getting paid every day, but I also had to be careful. I didn't know what would trigger the police or not. If I became official on legal documents, we could be found and that wasn't a risk I was prepared to take.

Not yet, at least.

Still, he was offering me a cash job and that was more than I could have hoped for. Zane seemed like a nice man and, hopefully, he wouldn't have a problem paying me under the table for a while.

I had no idea how long we would be staying here in town, but if there was no risk to us being found, and if I could have a stable job, I wasn't opposed to staying. It did feel like a town we could build a life in. I would have to see how it all went before I made any decisions on staying or not.

"I would appreciate the cash job," I said, flashing him a small smile.

"Do you have some time right now, and I can get you introduced to everyone and show you what we're doing?"

"Absolutely," I easily agreed.

Zane gave me a warm smile as he guided me out and started to show me around, introducing me to everyone. There were so many workers here, because Zane was building a resort, a rather large one based on the site. It was good, though, because that meant he would have work for easily a year or more before the site was finished. If we did decide to stay, I would have work for the year.

Afterward, I had no idea what I would

do. Unless there was some type of developer coming to town, I wouldn't have any work for myself. That could be a problem that I figured out later, though, should we decide to stay.

For now, I was going to be happy about having a job once again and someone that seemed reliable to watch River for me. This town might be small, but maybe it wasn't so bad to live here. I would have to look into rent prices and see if it was possible for me to save up and get a small one bedroom apartment. River could always have the bedroom and I could sleep in the living room.

I didn't care about myself. I just wanted a better life for River, one that he deserved. Maybe this was my chance at finally making that happen.

# CHAPTER THREE

Isaiah

THIS WAS THE part of my job that I hated. Today, we got the call from the police that they were going to do a raid on the tent city that the homeless community had constructed. It was illegal, but everyone in the city had ignored that fact. They were out on the outskirts and they weren't bothering anyone. However, the mayor was a complete asshole and he wanted to make sure the undesirable were never seen or spoken about.

I had been hoping there would be an election soon to try and get the mayor out of office, but it didn't look like anyone wanted to run against him. Without a competitor, there was no need for an election.

I wasn't happy about having to be here for this. Part of my job was to make sure that children were safe, but I hated knowing that if any children were here, I would have to take them into my care. They would become my client and I would need to make sure their parent or parents had a safe place for them to live before I could give the child back to them. I hated breaking up a family and it never went over well, rightfully so, with the parents. People who were homeless needed help, they didn't need more obstacles put in their way.

As the police started to show up and force the residents out of their sanctuary, I allowed my gaze to wander around the area. The police were at least letting the residents take down their tents and collect their things. Almost everyone was packing up, except one tent. I made my way over there, figuring that the occupant was sleeping. As I arrived at the tent, I saw different men packing things up, but one man was keeping his eyes on me. I gave him a warm and friendly smile as I spoke.

"Hi there, I'm Isaiah. Is anyone home here?" I asked, pointing to the tent.

"He's working. I'll take it down for

him," the man said with an edge to his voice.

I gave him a warm nod before I made my way around. I was trying to determine if any children were here. To my surprise, though, there weren't any. I had to give it to them, at least they were all single or couples without children. It made my day much easier to know that there were no children here. I stayed as everyone packed their things away, just in case a problem arose and I would be able to help.

When half of the camp was emptied, my roving gaze caught sight of the eyes of a child poking up from behind a pile of rocks just off in the distance. They were gone almost as fast as they came up and I knew whoever that was, they were watching until the coast was clear.

I made my way over to the rock pile and looked over to see a boy leaning against the rocks with his legs up against his chest. He looked about twelve to me and he was instantly looking up at me as I leaned over.

"Hello there. My name is Isaiah. What's yours?"

"My brother says to never talk to a stranger," the boy said back.

"That is very good advice," I said as I pulled out my badge to show him. "I work with the police to make sure that children are safe. It's okay, you can tell me your name, Buddy."

"He also says that you should make someone work to earn your name," he countered and I couldn't help but smirk.

Smart kid.

Smart brother.

"And how do I earn learning your name?"

"My name lies within the answer. I have a bed but I do not sleep. I have a mouth but I don't eat. You hear me whisper, but I never talk. You can see me run, yet I never walk. What am I?"

"I have to confess, I am terrible at riddles," I said.

This kid was something else. I really was terrible with riddles. I was never a puzzle person. I didn't do them and I couldn't make them. My brain wasn't wired that way. I was more mathematical. I didn't have a creative bone in my entire body.

"But it's so simple," he said, flashing me a warm smile.

"For you. You already know your name," I teased. "Can I have a hint?"

"Then you won't be working for it and, therefore, haven't earned it."

"Well, you're not wrong."

Damn this kid was smart and clever. He looked clean and healthy, too. He didn't look like he had been homeless. He wasn't underweight, his clothes were clean, and his hair and nails were as well. He didn't scream homeless kid to me.

"Are you lost?" I asked next.

"Nope, I always know where I am. As long as you can read the time from the sun and moon, and know where the North Star is, you're never lost. It's pretty simple, really."

"That is very true. But sometimes people get lost in a city, especially a new one. Are you new in town?" I asked next.

This boy was not a normal twelve year old, that I was certain of. He didn't look familiar and I knew a great deal of the children in town just through passing. Still, I could have easily missed him, but I didn't see how. He had shoulder length, straight, jet black hair, and deep brown eyes. His skin was slightly tanned and I immediately thought of Native American, maybe not full, but definitely at least half.

"Sort of," he said cryptically.

"I'm not going to get any type of a straight answer from you, am I?"

He just simply shrugged before he spoke. "Not until you learn my name."

"Fair enough, but I need you to come with me until we find your parents."

He was going to have to come with me whether he liked it or not. I couldn't leave him here. He would have to go back with me to work until I could find his parents. I wouldn't be able to do that until he actually told me his name. I would get it eventually, though, even if I had to ask people at work what the riddle meant.

He didn't want to go with me, I could see it all over his face, but he also knew he didn't have much of a choice in the matter. He stood and easily followed me back to my car. I got him settled inside the back seat and climbed into the driver's seat. Driving carefully over the rutted ground until we reached the highway, I pulled out onto the paved road and headed toward town and for my office.

Glancing into the rearview a couple of times, I saw him keeping his gaze out the window as the different buildings passed us by. He didn't say anything and I was perfectly fine with it. We didn't need to talk and I suspected he knew where he was going. He was smart. He would have known what my badge meant.

After we pulled up to the building, I parked my car in my assigned spot and we both climbed out. I guided him inside and over to one of the private rooms that we used to talk to the children. The room had a two-way mirror as well so I would be able to watch as Dr. Holland spoke with my little charge.

Whenever a new child was brought into the system, Dr. Holland had to speak with them to ensure they weren't a danger to themselves or someone else.

"Make yourself comfortable, Buddy," I said as we walked into the room.

The room itself wasn't a typical interview room. It was designed for kids and to make them feel more comfortable. There was a small table where the younger kids could sit to play or color. There were also a couple of comfortable chairs for the older kids to enjoy. There were toys, coloring materials, and books for every age.

The young man went and sat down in one of the chairs and looked right at me. Most kids tended to wander around and check the room out, but this kid was not having it. He was acting more like an adult than he was a kid.

"You know, if you told me your name, I could call your parents," I offered.

"You would know it already if you could solve a simple riddle," he countered.

Little smart ass.

Dr. Holland would get his name from him. I had no doubt that he would be able to decode his little riddle. Before I could even respond, Dr. Holland was interrupting us, thankfully.

"This is Dr. Holland. He is just going to speak with you for a few minutes," I said.

"I don't need a Shrink," the young man instantly said.

"I am merely a psychologist," Dr. Holland stated.

"Which are therapists, therefore, a Shrink. You want to psychoanalyze me to determine if all of my mental facilities are in check or if I am a potential danger to you, myself, or another child. Saying you are a psychologist doesn't change what you do."

"Well, that was impressive. Those were some big words for a kid your age. You are what, twelve?" Dr. Holland asked, flashing a warm smile as he moved into the room.

"My age doesn't reflect my IQ level and

it's foolish and patronizing for an adult to assume that due to my age I am incapable of making valid and logical arguments or form opinions."

I couldn't help but smile and glance over at Dr. Holland. He was just as surprised as I was.

This kid had to be gifted.

There was just no other way.

"Ask him his name," I said.

"He can't figure it out," the boy pointed out.

"Well, I would be happy to give it a shot," Dr. Holland said easily as he sat down on one of the chairs.

"I have a bed but I do not sleep. I have a mouth but I don't eat. You hear me whisper, but I never talk. You can see me run, yet I never walk. What am I?"

I looked over at Dr. Holland and

watched as he sat there for a moment thinking before he finally spoke. "It's nice to meet you, River."

"Are you serious?" I asked. There was no way he figured it out that fast.

"You didn't get it?" Dr. Holland asked me, slightly surprised.

"I don't do riddles or puzzles."

"Even very basic ones, apparently," River commented.

"Okay, I'm going to leave you two alone."

I headed out and made my way over into the connecting room. I now had his first name, but I needed a last name to be able to run it. Even with a less common name like River, it would still come back with quite a few. This kid, though, was smart and well cared for, so someone was out there looking for him.

They had to be.

Of course, that was assuming anyone even knew he was missing. His parents could easily think he was at school or the library, right now. My gut was telling me, though, something else was going on. Because if he was supposed to be in school or at the library, he would have just said it.

Someone taught him to be street smart.

Someone taught him to not give his name.

Someone taught him when to hide and when to not fight.

"So, River, can you tell me where your parents are?" Dr. Holland started.

"I don't know where they are."

"I'm only trying to help you, River. I want to make sure you get back to your parents. Could you help me out a bit here, please?" Dr. Holland asked calmly.

"I can't give you an answer that I don't know. My parents are out in the world somewhere, I'm sure, but I don't know where or if they are even alive, to be honest. Though, I guess even dead they could still be out in the world. That would depend on what your spiritual beliefs are. I prefer science, but that's just me," River said with a small shrug.

"Understandable. Someone takes care of you, though. I can tell that you are well fed, you are dressed in clean clothes, your body is clean. You certainly don't look like someone that lives in a homeless encampment."

"I am very well taken care of," River easily agreed.

"But who takes care of you? I

understand you might not wish to talk to me or anyone here. However, if we don't know who is taking care of you, then we will have no choice but to put you into a foster home. That is the very last thing any of us wants. So, please, can you tell me who looks after you?" Dr. Holland said with a great deal of patience. He was always amazing with children. It was why we used him full-time.

I saw River let out a small huff and I knew he was debating on what to do. For some reason, he didn't want to give up who was looking after him and it didn't make much sense. If he was already in foster care, then he would have said so. If he was being looked after by a relative, then he could have easily said so. It was weird that he wasn't giving it up so freely and that had put a bad feeling in the pit of my stomach. After a moment River spoke.

"My brother, Sol, takes care of me."

"Okay, and how old is Sol?" Dr. Holland asked.

"He's nineteen."

"And was he there at the tent city?"

"Nope."

"Where is he, then, River?"

"He was looking to get a job. We're new in town and he thought he could get a job at the construction site."

So they were new. I figured as much. I would have remembered seeing them, their Native American traits stood out in this town. Chances were, they were living in the tent city, probably the tent that was left unoccupied.

"And you both live in the tent city?" Dr. Holland asked.

"Why does that matter?" River asked, clearly feeling defensive.

"We just want to make sure you are safe and properly cared for, River, that's all."

"You literally just finished saying that I was well fed, clean, and taken care of. Now you want to question whether or not my brother is doing a good job. Why? Because you think we're homeless so that must mean he's an alcoholic or a drug addict? Or maybe because we're Native American, and that must mean he is incapable of working hard. Your stereotypes are not appreciated."

This wasn't working. River was getting defensive and I knew that meant he would shut down. If we wanted to get anything out of him, we had to do this a bit differently. I headed out of the room and into their room.

"How about we grab a snack, River?" I asked.

I could tell Dr. Holland was confused and slightly annoyed that I was interrupting him, but I needed to get River to feel more comfortable and I had a feeling he wasn't going to be comfortable remaining in this room.

River gave a small shrug, but that was good enough for me. He got up and I guided him out of the room with a small nod to Dr. Holland to let him know we would be okay. I took him into the small break room.

"Do you like chips or chocolate?" I asked.

"Sol says it's important to not eat too much sugar or your teeth will fall out. Do you have any apples?" he asked as he slid into a chair.

"We do."

I found it interesting that River was more interested in an apple than chocolate, but I had to give respect to Sol. He had somehow managed to get a soon-to-be teenager to eat fruit over junk food. I handed him the apple as I sat down across the table from him.

"Apples are good for your brain. Did you know that apples are a leading source of quercetin? It's an antioxidant plant chemical that keeps your mental juices flowing by protecting your brain cells. Some scientific studies have shown that people who eat apples at least once a day can help to reduce the onset of neurodegenerative diseases, like Alzheimer's and Parkinson's. It's also good to help control blood sugar, prevent heart disease and some forms of cancer." The young man quoted the information like he'd memorized a medical book. I was impressed, to say the least.

"Wow, I did not know that. I'll have to pick up some apples tonight on my way home. How do you know that?"

"Sol takes me to the library all the time. He lets me spend as much time there as I want to read. He never complains once about the hours that we spend there. Even though he takes me there so I can be more social with kids my own age and not to read."

"He sounds like a good brother. River, I am going to be straight with you and talk to you like I would an adult. I think you are very smart and there is no point in me talking down to you or trying to sugarcoat anything," I started.

"I can respect that," River agreed, and took a bite of the apple.

"I don't want to put you into the foster system. That is the last thing that I want. And I really don't want to take you away from your brother. He seems like he is doing a great job with you. If you have nowhere to live, I can help you with that. I need to talk to your brother, though, so I can make that happen. I'm not looking to take you away from him. Is there a way I can reach him?"

"He'll come here. He had to go and see about a job at the construction site but then he will go back to the tent city. Once he sees that it's gone, he'll talk to Max and then come here."

"Who is Max?"

"The man that lives next to us, or he did live next to us. He was keeping an eye on me and told me to run once the police started to pull in. He's a nice man. He's been teaching me Spanish," River said, flashing a warm smile.

"I actually know Spanish. You seem like a kid that just loves to learn anything."

"I've always loved to learn. Sol teaches me everything he knows. Life is all about learning everything you can so you can try and change the world."

"What about friends, though?"

"I make friends in every city we've lived in, but they are all older. Kids my age are kinda dumb. Sol says it's not nice to say that, but it's also not nice to lie."

"He's right, it's not nice to say mean things, but I can also understand where you are coming from. You are very smart for your age. How often do you change cities?”

“Every six months.”

I didn’t like that part. It was vital for children to have stability and not know where they were going to be putting their head down at night. Traveling from one town to the next and, at that fast of a pace, wasn’t good for a child. It didn’t help promote a healthy and stable environment.

“How do you feel about that?”

“It doesn’t bother me as long as we have each other. Sol does everything he can to keep me and take care of me. He takes very good care of me. He said once we find the right town, we’ll settle down, and then I’ll be able to go to school. Maybe that will be this town.”

“Would you like to stay here?”

“It seems like an okay town. I don’t

know. We just got here less than a week ago. If he gets a good job, then we might be able to stay longer."

That was the trick. If Sol was able to get a job at the construction site that would keep him employed for at least a year. That might be enough to get them back on their feet.

I would have to talk to Sol and see what his plan was and what was going on. I had a feeling there was more to this situation than River was either telling me or that he knew.

It wasn't uncommon for the homeless community to move around, however, they didn't run from town to town every six months, especially with a child. I would be keeping an eye on River and Sol. I would reserve judgment until I had a reason to doubt Sol's ability to take care of River.

Hopefully, Sol would be here soon and I would be able to talk to him about what had been going on. Maybe I would be able to get more out of Sol than I did River. I just hoped that Sol didn't want to ask me a riddle, too.

# CHAPTER FOUR

Sol

BY THE TIME I arrived back at the tent camp, I was completely conflicted on what to do. Part of me wanted to stay here in town and try to build a life for myself and River.

If it had just been me, I wouldn't have cared. I would happily travel around the country chasing different jobs. It would be an easy life for me and I would be able to see the country and experience new experiences. However, River deserved to have a stable life, and for the past four years I had been failing him in that regard.

I hated that I had been failing him.

I hated that he wasn't able to have friends his own age. That he couldn't go to school or even be able to have his own bedroom. I wanted him to have more than we had with our parents, not less.

The only thing that was going for me was the fact that River hadn't been hurt. I had been able to protect him from Phillip and any other pervert out there that wanted to touch him. I was not about to fail him in that area, no matter what I had to do.

I would have to wait and see how this

job went and if it was possible for me to work on paper, then I always could. I needed to get a feel for the town as well. We definitely stood out here and I wasn't too sure if that would be a good or a bad thing.

Racism lived all over this country and we had both experienced it in our travels over the past four years. I wasn't about to settle down in any town where I would have to worry about River being attacked because his skin was darker. Everything was up in the air and I wouldn't know what to do until some time had gone by.

The second I arrived at where the tent camp was supposed to be, my stomach went straight up into my throat.

The tents were gone.

Everyone was gone.

I had no idea where River had gone or

where our stuff was. I had no idea that the police would be coming to move the tent city and I knew it was the police. We had gone through it before where the police raided the camp. However, based on what some of the others were telling me, the town didn't have a problem with the tent city.

I had to find River.

He knew what to do if he saw the police, he was to hide and not come out unless I went to get him. He was to hide somewhere nearby so I could easily find him, but to make sure he hid well enough that the police wouldn't find him.

I instantly started to walk around, checking into small hiding spots wherever I thought River would have gone. It was only a few minutes into my search when I saw Max coming toward me.

"Sol, River's not here," Max said.

"Did you get him?"

I was praying that Max had been able to get River out of there before the police got a hold of him. The very last thing I needed was them finding out he was a missing child.

I didn't have proof that we were labeled as missing, but if Phillip wanted to keep getting his checks, he would have to tell the social worker that we were missing. Otherwise, it wouldn't have looked good when she showed up for her monthly checks to find out we weren't there. If the police ran River's prints or his photo, they would have found the case file and he could be shipped off back to Phillip.

Something I couldn't allow to happen.

"No. I saw the police pull up too late. I got him to run and he hid behind that rock formation, but a social worker got him. He was taken to the social services building."

"Fuck," I said. I rubbed my hands over my face.

The social service building was the worst place for him to have gone. They would definitely run his name and prints and they would discover he was missing.

They would be looking for me to press charges.

Even if they didn't run his name, if River was able to delay them and keep them guessing, there was nothing I could do about us being homeless. The social worker would know we were living in a tent and they could put River into the foster system. I had to try and prevent that, but if the worker didn't want to work with me on it, there was nothing I could do.”

“It'll be okay. It was Isaiah. He's a really good guy and very fair. He's worked with a few other homeless parents before and he didn't break them up. He just wants to make sure kids are safe,” Max advised.

“In my experience, that doesn't normally happen.”

It sure as shit didn't happen with us, but I guess both of our parents were unfit to handle one child, much less two. If I could show that I could be a good parent to River, then maybe this Isaiah guy wouldn't take him from me. The problem was, I had no idea what he was going to do until I went and actually spoke with him.

“Where is our stuff?”

Not that I cared too much about some

of it, but I didn't want to lose the tent or any of River's items. He had a few books that he loved and would reread every week.

"I have it. We're all setting up camp about two miles from here just on the outskirts of the town."

"Thank you, I appreciate that," I said warmly.

Max didn't have to grab our things. He could have left them to be taken away by the cops or for someone else to grab them. He was a good man and it meant a lot to me that he was helping.

"No worries. You go and get River. I'll hold onto your stuff."

I gave a nod and headed off for the social services building. I knew where it was because I always made sure to know where the police station and social services were located in every new town. I made sure to avoid them like the plague and River knew to avoid them as well.

We hadn't been in a town this small before and maybe that was my mistake. We had been living in larger towns because it was easier to stay hidden. For the longest time, I was certain that someone was coming for us, but no one ever did.

Bigger cities, though, came with problems.

There was a lot more competition for cash jobs. There were more police, more homeless people, more violence, and more issues within the homeless communities. I had always been able to find a nice person to watch River when I did get work, but I would be lying if I said I hadn't been worried the whole time. You just never know when someone's mental illness would hit them and they could have hurt River.

Thankfully, that never happened.

When we came here, I wasn't expecting to stay too long. We would be gone within six months, but we should have stayed only a few nights before we moved on. If we had, then River wouldn't be in the care of social services and I might not be potentially going to prison.

I just prayed that they didn't run his name or his fingerprints. I couldn't risk River going into the foster system again, there was no telling what someone could do to him. He was twelve and that was the perfect age for a lot of child molesters.

I needed to get River and get the hell out of town with him. His safety was my top priority and I was not going to let anyone take him from me. Not after everything we had been through.

It took a good twenty minutes before I arrived at social services. I had to take a five minute breather before I physically went into the building.

I had to look like I could take care of him.

I had to show this Isaiah guy that I would be trusted with the child.

The one thing going for me was the fact that I always made sure we were both clean. I always washed our clothes in various ponds or lakes, any body of water that I could. We were both always bathed and our hair was brushed. I kept my long hair in a braid to make it easier to keep clean. I always made sure River ate properly and wouldn't get sick.

River was too young to remember most

of what our mother taught us, but I remembered all of the tricks that she had been taught by her parents. With being Native American, we knew how to eat from the Earth and how to live off of the land. That knowledge had helped to keep us looking like normal citizens and not homeless people.

I walked in the building and immediately felt on edge. I hadn't been in one of these buildings since I was eleven when we were taken away from our mother.

That hadn't been a pleasant experience.

Even though our mother was not good for us, we still didn't want to leave her. I didn't want to leave her. I had been taking care of River from the day he was born, but I had also been taking care of our mother for just as long.

It was me that made sure she ate and didn't choke when she passed out drunk. It was me that cleaned her up and made her presentable when the social worker would pop in.

It was me that got River ready for school and made sure he was fed. It was me skipping school to work for cash doing various jobs so we would have food in the house that week.

I had been doing it all since I was only seven.

Then, we had been taken away and put with Phillip, and for that first month I had felt free. For the first time in four years, I wasn't the adult. I got to be a kid, too. I didn't have to worry about making sure there was food in the house. I didn't have to worry about making meals. I could go to school just like River and have friends.

I hated Phillip, but the thing was, even while he was molesting me, I was still happy that I didn't have to take care of River by myself anymore. Phillip still made sure we had everything we ever needed.

I knew there was a psychological trauma I'd suffered in that, and the reason why I couldn't fully hate him. I knew it was because he still took care of us, took care of River, and gave me the freedom to be a kid, for the first time in my life, really. Still, some days I felt like something was wrong with me because I couldn't fully hate him.

"Hello there, how may I help you?" the receptionist asked, snapping me out of my thoughts.

"I am here to see Isaiah. He found my brother."

"Can I have your name, please?"

"Sol."

"I'll let him know," the receptionist said, flashing me a warm smile as she picked up the phone.

I moved over toward the waiting area, but I didn't sit down. I kept my gaze on the bulletin boards of all the different parenting classes, drug classes, daycares, and play groups that they had going on in the town. I did notice that most of them were all within the same building.

I don't know why, but the drug classes surprised me. I would have figured a town this size wouldn't have that high of a drug addict population. This town was smaller, but not miniature. Still though, almost everyone that I saw was working.

This was a working town of middle class to high end society. They didn't have any undesirables, and if they did, they kept them hidden away like the homeless. It was a town designed to keep the poor, poor and the rich, rich.

"You must be Sol," a deep male voice came from behind me.

I turned to see a man in his thirties with a neatly trimmed beard and brown hair with brown eyes. He was a bit larger. It wasn't a beer gut, but more of a gut that you get from eating well and not having the time to work it off. He was average looking, but I knew better than to judge a book by its cover. He could easily be a horrible person or a teddy bear. I knew better than to make assumptions about people.

People had made assumptions about

Phillip and I knew how that turned out.

"Isaiah?" I asked.

"It's nice to meet you," he said as he held his hand out.

I easily took it as I spoke. "Where's my brother?"

"He's in the break room. If you come with me, we can chat a bit."

He made it sound like I had the choice of saying no, but I knew I didn't. If I said no, he would never let me have River and that was all that mattered to me. I simply gave a nod and followed him through the small building until we reached an interview room. This was not going to be easy and I was not going to like what he had to say. Thankfully, I had one trick up my sleeve.

"I need to talk to you about River. He informed me that you both are homeless,"

Isaiah began.

"That's not a crime," I instantly said.

"I'm not saying it is. However, it's my job to make sure that the children in this town are taken care of properly. Being homeless is not an ideal situation for a child."

"We're new in town and still looking to settle in. We're protected by Native law. You can't remove him from my care unless you are able to place him in a foster home with another Native American. I haven't been in your town for very long, but I know we are the only Natives in town. Legally, you can't take him."

That was the only thing keeping River in my care here. I knew for a fact that he couldn't remove River from me unless he was placed with another Native. It didn't work with us all the time because this law was not nationwide. It only existed in certain States, but that's why we had only lived in those States since we left Phillip.

"I know the law, and I never said I was taking him from you. The very last thing I want to do is break up a family. However, I need to talk to you to gather more information on your situation. Once we are done, you can sign some paperwork and then leave with River," Isaiah said calmly.

I didn't fully believe him, but Max had said that Isaiah wasn't interested in breaking up families. I also didn't have much of a choice. Even though Native Law protected us, Isaiah could have sent River to another town for a foster home if he felt like I wasn't good enough for River.

Or if he discovered what our last name

was and that I had actually kidnapped him.

I had to play his game right now.

"What do you want to know?"

"How old are you?" Isaiah asked as he opened his notebook.

"Nineteen. River is twelve."

"And how long have you been caring for River on your own?"

This was the tricky part, because I had no idea what River had already told him. I had to be careful, but if I lied too much that would hurt me in the long run. It wasn't a crime to have bad parents, but if he discovered that we had been on our own for four years, that would make him look into us and I couldn't have that.

"Since I was eighteen. Our parents weren't stable, so we left."

"And you have been homeless since?"

"We have been, but we know how to live off of the land. River's always had food to eat and a place to sleep that was safe. I take very good care of him."

"I'm not doubting that. He looks very well taken care of and he is incredibly smart. I'm not judging you, Sol. If it wasn't safe at home with your parents for River, you did the right thing by taking him with you. I'm not about to penalize you for protecting your little brother. I am here to help you. I am here to help River. I'm not the enemy. He will be placed back in your care, however, I will still be involved. I will be doing weekly check ins with you both to make sure progress is being made."

"What progress?"

I didn't like that sound of that and I really didn't like that he would still be in our lives. That meant we couldn't leave, because then it would be reported to the police and shit would hit the fan. I would have to wait to take River away until Isaiah was no longer poking around in our lives.

"You will need to find stable housing for you and River. You need to have a job so you can financially support him. And River needs to be enrolled in a school. There is a motel that we work with for those that are homeless. I can give you a voucher for a free week stay, then after that you will need to pay three hundred for the week every Saturday. There is housing in town, but it doesn't often come up so when you do see an apartment come up you will want to jump on it. I can also help you try and locate suitable housing as well. As long as you agree to the terms, you can have River in your care."

It wasn't like I had any choice in the matter. My back was up against the wall and I had no choice but to agree to it. I was just hoping I would be able to make it all happen and get rid of Isaiah as quickly as possible. The longer he was in our lives, the higher the risk of him discovering the truth about who we are and why we left. I wasn't going to risk that getting out. Even if I wasn't at risk of being arrested for kidnapping, I was not about to let anyone know what Phillip had done to me.

I'd take that to my grave.

"What do I need to sign?" I just wanted to get this over and done with.

Isaiah handed me the paperwork and after I read through it all, I signed my life away. With that done, Isaiah put all of the paperwork away in his folder. With that done, I was about to get up, but stopped when he spoke.

"I'm sorry for asking you this, but I have to know. Your eyes are blue."

That was not the first time someone had asked me about my eyes. River had brown eyes, everyone in our family did. All Native Americans had brown eyes and black hair, that was a trait that none of us could escape. Yet, I was born with sky blue eyes. People always asked me about them and assumed I had been a half-breed, as they liked to call me. The truth was, it was just science.

"I have a mutated gene that changed my eye color."

"It makes you very unique," he said warmly.

I didn't feel unique.

Living around other Natives, I always felt like an outcast because of it. It was something that made me stand out, and when you were trying to avoid doing just that, it was not a good position to be in.

Natives tended to be very spiritual and superstitious. My mother hated my eyes. She believed that the devil's spirit had infiltrated her body while pregnant with me. She had gone as far as performing exorcisms on me to change my eye color. She always blamed her drinking on me to go with it.

It was hard not to take personally, even though as I got older I knew she was only using my eyes as an excuse to drink and not take proper care of us.

Still, it hurt.

"Where's my brother?" I asked. I didn't

want to make small talk with him any longer than necessary.

"Right this way," he said, flashing me a warm smile once again.

I wasn't certain why he was being so nice. Most of the time authorities had a problem with Natives. They considered us to be trouble. Always smoking, drinking, and doing nothing to improve society.

We had a bad rep and it was one that seemed to be Nationwide, from my experiences. Isaiah was being nice, far too nice for my comfort level, and it made me even more suspicious.

The sooner I got River out of here, the better.

He guided me over to their break room where I saw River sitting down reading a book.

"Hey are you all right, Bear?" I asked

as I bent down in front of him. I did a quick scan of his body and I didn't see any injuries or distress.

"I'm okay. Can we leave now?" He didn't enjoy being here any more than I did. He was old enough to know that I would be in trouble should anyone discover our story.

"Absolutely," I easily agreed.

"Here is the voucher for the motel. It is Lighthouse Inn and just ten minutes from here. I will see you both in a week and will be in touch," Isaiah said as he handed me the voucher.

"Thank you," I said as I took the voucher and started to guide River out of there.

I didn't breathe easier until we got outside and down the block. Now that we were finally free from the building, I could stop worrying about someone grabbing River and dragging him away from me.

That fear would be there later when I would have to figure out how to afford the motel. Even working for cash, I wouldn't be able to make three hundred for the motel in seven days. I would need to supplement it with other work and that was something I was not looking forward to.

"Is everything okay?" River asked.

"Everything is fine. We are going to be staying at a motel for the week. Let's go and see Max to get our stuff before we check in."

"An actual motel, that's awesome," River said with a huge smile that didn't warm my heart. Instead, it sent a sharp pain through it. He should not be that happy to be able to sleep on a bed.

# TORMENTED

I had to do better for him.

# CHAPTER FIVE

Sol

IT WAS NEARING eight o'clock at night and I was dressed to head out.

After we had seen Max and grabbed our things, we headed straight for the motel. The room had two double beds and it was decent. There was hot water and even a television for River. He hadn't been able to watch television since we left

Phillip's house four years ago.

I had used what little money we had left to grab some food for us. Just a few things that we would be able to keep in the small fridge in the room. I needed to go out tonight to make some cash to be able to afford to live here. At least, until I started to get steady money through the construction site. If I signed the paperwork to be a legal worker I would make double the money, but I would have to wait two weeks to receive it. For the next two weeks, whether I liked it or not, I would have to work the streets to make enough money for us to live here and to give River the food he needed.

"Okay, I'm going to head out. You're sure you are okay to stay here alone?" I asked.

I knew he was twelve and he didn't

need a babysitter. Still, he had always stayed with someone when I went to work. Though, then we were living on the streets and it wasn't really safe to leave him alone. Now, he was in a motel room that had two locks on the door. He would be safe here for a few hours. I only needed to make fifty dollars a night, which was one guy. I would only be an hour or so. I would be back long before he needed to get some sleep.

"I told you I would be fine. I'll lock the door and stay in here. I'll even close the blinds, if that makes you feel better," River offered.

"It would. Okay, I'll be back within two hours. Lock up behind me," I said as I grabbed the room key and stuffed it in my pants pocket.

I closed the door behind me and didn't

actually leave until I heard both locks engage and saw that he closed all of the blinds and curtains over the windows. With my brother safe inside the motel room, I strolled down to where the majority of the prostitutes went. I just needed to get this over and done with and then I could get back to River.

# CHAPTER SIX

Isaiah

I MADE MY way down the street to meet Dominic at a coffee shop. I was hoping he would be able to help with getting a group home built for all of the children the task force was bringing back to town. I decided to walk instead of driving because it was only a five minute walk and it was nice out.

I was trying to walk more. I needed the exercise, that was for sure. I knew I had to try and lose some weight to ensure my health wouldn't take a hit from all of the food I'd been eating, especially now that I was getting older and my metabolism kept slowing more and more.

I was not going to step foot into a gym, but my doctor had said walking every day would be good. I did spend a lot of my day and night sitting down working away on my cases, so the added exercise would be good all around.

I had been trying to work last night, but I couldn't stop thinking about River and Sol. Especially Sol. I had never seen a man as beautiful as him. His skin was a rich tan color, and his long, straight jet black hair looked like silk as it flowed down his back in a single braid. I bet if I ran my fingers through his loose locks they would glide right though. He was fit, too. I could tell he worked with his hands and was not shy about hard labor. I had to imagine his body underneath his clothes was remarkable.

It was his eyes, though, that haunted my thoughts. They were breathtaking. I had never seen eyes that blue before and never had I seen anyone of his ethnicity with blue eyes. It made him so unique, but also gorgeous.

I discovered that I was gay in my final year of getting my Master's Degree. It was an accident. My roommate dragged me out to this frat party and I ended up getting drunk kissed by this one guy.

That was my first kiss.

Some guy, whose name I still don't know, had grabbed me and kissed me.

It was not memorable at all.

It wasn't anything special like a first kiss was supposed to be. However, I did discover that, as sloppy as it was, I did enjoy it.

Growing up, I just didn't seem to have any interest in sex or relationships like other people my age did. It didn't bother me, either. All through high school I was too busy with schoolwork to care.

In university, I was focused on bettering myself, and my life. I was going to school, working part time, and focusing all of my energy on getting my Master's with a plan to go into social work. That didn't leave a whole lot of time for anything else, anyway. Sexual activity didn't mean anything to me and even after being kissed and discovering I preferred men, I still really hadn't done much.

I had two boyfriends in my life, but they never lasted long. They were very interested in sex, but for me it wasn't a high priority. We fooled around, but never made it past our hands. I had never received or given oral, and intercourse was completely off the table.

I knew it was a combination of my childhood and how I was raised coupled with my own self-esteem issues. I didn't exactly look amazing with my shirt off. I was self-conscious and I always felt like the two guys I had dated were disappointed in my appearance.

Not to mention my inexperience, as well.

That was a huge annoyance to them, because they saw no need to wait to have sex. To them, they didn't need a real connection with someone to have sex.

Whereas to me, sex was supposed to be special.

It was something to be shared with another person that you care deeply for. It was something that shouldn't be treated as an easy transaction, as if you were asking for a slice of bread from someone.

I wanted something more.

I wanted to feel a spiritual connection with my partner, and until that happened, I was not willing to give up my virginity.

I was looking forward to seeing Sol and River again, though. I wanted to make sure that they were doing okay and I was very interested in getting to know both of them more.

And I felt a strong desire to help River.

He was a very bright boy and I could

tell he would thrive in a private school setting. I was hoping with an IQ test he would be able to obtain a full-scholarship with the private school in the area. He would do very well with the school and they would be able to help him adjust and get socialized with the other children. It would be hard for him in a normal school with his intelligence. Kids his age were interested in the opposite sex, video games, and comic books. River didn't come across as the type of child that was interested in any of that, at least not right now. Private school would be the best solution for River and for his future school career.

I'd bet my career on it.

Once I arrived at the coffee shop, I headed inside and quickly grabbed a coffee before making my way over to where Dominic was sitting. He gave me a warm smile as he stood and held his hand out for me.

"It's nice to officially meet you, Isaiah."

"It's nice to meet you, Dominic. Travis speaks very highly of you," I said as I grasped his hand.

"Travis is a great guy," he said as we sat down.

"He is. We are very lucky to have him with the agency."

Travis was one of the newer hires, but he fit in very well. We had become good friends and I was hoping he would start to open up to me more. As of right now, I had no idea where he lived, what his personal life was like, if he had any family.

Hell, I didn't even know what his favorite color was.

At work, he was always professional and outside of work he kept his walls up. I knew some people took more time to get used to a new work environment, but I was hoping soon Travis would feel more comfortable and let people in to his world, to get to know him.

"He said you were hoping to talk to me about getting a group home started?" Dominic inquired.

"We are, yes. As you may be aware, we now have a task force in town, working to help stop crimes against children. They were originally brought in when the corruption within the foster system was exposed. They have stayed to continue to help as many children as possible. Travis and I work with them, and when there are children found, we bring them back here. Some can be placed with family and others need to go to a foster home. We have been working with other towns to secure proper placements. However, we are reaching our capacity limits. We would like to have a group home built for the children."

"First, I applaud you for your help with the task force and helping to protect children. They are the most vulnerable and should always be protected. This group home, are you looking to have it where it's a temporary stop until you find a permanent place for them, or to have it run by someone to keep the children there?"

"A bit of both. Ideally, we would like to use it as a safe haven for the children that have no loved ones they can go to and might not fit well in a foster home. As you can imagine, some of the children we have rescued have been horribly abused and they don't always do well in foster homes. They need a great deal of therapy and a more hands-on adult that is trained on how to handle their trauma. The task force isn't slowing down any time soon. Just as soon as they shut down one human trafficking ring, another takes its place. We're trying to prevent children falling through the cracks and we don't want to flood the foster homes that we do have, because then the quality of child care goes down."

It was a hard place to be right now for us. We didn't want to stress the foster homes that we did have with having too many children. It's why we had limited it to three children per home, regardless of how many children they felt they could handle.

Too many children and the stress becomes too much.

We were trying to avoid having children moving from one home to the next. Ideally, once a child was placed within that home, that was their home until they turned eighteen. We were getting to the point of having too many children who needed help and all of the foster homes in the ten towns around us were starting to get tight as well. We needed more foster homes. We were already looking at working with other cities to try and keep some kids local. It was still a mess and a lot of red tape to work through.

"I think it's a great idea. I would be happy to help you with it and to introduce you to some investors, as well. I know quite a few businessmen that are in need of a charity write off, as long as you don't get offended by it, they will be happy to donate," Dominic said with a small shrug.

"As long as the check clears, I don't care about the reason for their donation."

I knew in order for large businesses to survive during tax time they had to make charitable donations. If those donations went toward these kids, I had no problem with it. Money was money and that was all that mattered.

"That's the perfect attitude to have about it. I'll reach out to them. Do you need any help getting it started?"

"If you wouldn't mind pointing us in the right direction for that, that would be great. We've never had to do something like this before."

It was one thing to say that you want to build a group home and another to actually know how to make that possible. There would be regulations we would need to go through and try to work out. It was going to be a huge undertaking, but it was one we needed to take on.

"I can work with you on it and get it going. The mayor also really likes me so I'll get him on board. Jason, he works as the foreman on Zane's resort, and he runs his own construction company. He'll probably have workers willing to help with building, as well. He would also know which buildings in town could be transformed into a group home. We might be able to avoid having to build one from scratch." Dominic flashed me a smile.

"Wow, that would be great. Thank you so much. I truly appreciate it." Excitement laced my voice.

This was more than we could have

asked for. Travis had said that Dominic was a good man, but I didn't expect for him to be willing to help us this much. He also had connections to people in construction, making this even easier. It was almost too good to be true, but I trusted Travis and if he said that Dominic was solid, that was good enough for me.

"It's no problem. Children deserve to grow up as children. They aren't supposed to know that monsters truly exist in the world. If we fail them as adults, it's on us to make them better. I'm happy to help."

I was thankful for his help. It was going to take a lot of us working together for us to get this group home up and running. I was excited about getting it started and, hopefully, within the year we would have this group home up and running.

# CHAPTER SEVEN

Isaiah

I SAUNTERED MY way up to Damien's office. We had gotten to know each other while being on the task force. Damien and Sebastian were private detectives, but they often helped with locating different suspects or victims that the task force were not able to locate.

The task force worked a lot of cases

and it helped to have two registered private detectives to work the other cases to gather more actionable intel. It freed up the task force to go after the criminals that they did have solid intel on.

I had been speaking with Damien on the side about locating any of my other siblings or relatives. I wanted to make sure that I didn't have any relatives that were in need of help. If they were looking to get out of the FLDS, I would be more than willing to help make that happen.

"Isaiah, didn't expect to see you here," Damien said as he walked toward his office.

"I know you're busy, I just wanted to stop in on my way home to see if you had anything," I said as I followed him into his office.

"Nothing for the task force, but I did

locate a younger brother of yours.”

“Is he okay?”

My siblings used to all live in one home with my mother, but after her death ten years ago, they were now spread out all over different FLDS compounds in various states. They weren't really living with relatives so it was harder to track them down.

“He appeared to be fine. As you know, our guys can't get too close. He's fifteen and working on a farm. We have feelers out for anyone that is looking to escape, but no biters yet.”

“Okay, well, I appreciate you keeping an eye out for me.”

He didn't have to be doing the extra investigating, and he certainly didn't have to be doing it for free. I greatly appreciated his help in all of this.

"They're children. They don't belong in a cult. Any of my guys would say the same thing."

They were all good men that Damien hired. I had yet to meet any of them, but that was by design. Damien liked to keep his men a secret. It made it easier for them to go into different areas without the threat of being recognized.

I had no idea what he did outside of the task force, but I suspected I didn't want to know. As long as Damien was one of the good guys, I didn't care to ask too many questions.

"Still, I appreciate it. Next time at the bar, it's on me," I promised.

"Deal," Damien easily agreed.

I wasn't much of a drinker, but I could have one or two when the occasion called for it. Normally, after a very large bust that saved a lot of children, that's when I would sit with the guys and have a couple. For tonight, I would be going back home to get more work done. I would see Sol and River again in six days and I needed to make sure my head was on straight for it. I just hoped that six days was enough to get his blue eyes out of my mind.

# CHAPTER EIGHT

Sol

TODAY WAS MY first shift at the construction site. I had just dropped River off with Max for the day at the new tent city location. I wasn't sure what they were going to be doing today, but River seemed excited to be learning more Spanish from him. Max had offered to do it for free, but I refused and would be giving him some money for today. He would be watching River for eight hours, so the least I could do was give him something.

I had been out for an hour last night before I came back to the motel. I immediately took a shower to try and get the feeling of the man's rough hands and smell off of me.

I'd had to sell my body before, mostly in the beginning when we were first trying to figure it all out. I hated every single second of it. I never got pleasure out of the touch of another man. Even when Phillip had tried to get me aroused, it never happened.

At first, I figured I wasn't into guys, but once I hit puberty I would have wet dreams and they were always about two guys. I never fantasized about a woman. I was gay, which made it easier to sell my body when I needed the cash, but it didn't make it any easier to handle the fact that I was tainted and broken.

I would never be able to have a real relationship with a man because they would never be able to understand what I had been through. No man would ever want me after what I had been through and had had happen to me, anyway.

I had accepted that my life would always be focused on making sure River was taken care of. Once he turned eighteen, I figured I still wouldn't be dating anyone. I was going to be alone for the rest of my life and there was nothing I could do about it.

"Sol!" A male voice called out.

I looked over and saw Zane and another man standing by the trailer. Zane waved me over and I made my way to them. I hoped that Zane was not about to tell me I couldn't work there any more. I really needed this job, otherwise, I would have to work more at night and that was the last thing I wanted to be doing.

"Boss," I acknowledged with a nod to Zane.

"Sol, I want you to meet Jason. He's my foreman and will be working closely with you until you learn the ropes," Zane said.

"It's nice to meet you, Sol." Jason held his hand out and I easily took it as he spoke.

"You, too," I said back, breathing an inward sigh of relief.

"All right, I will leave you two alone to get sorted out. Sol, come see me at the end of your shift for your pay," Zane said, flashing me a friendly smile.

"Sure thing, Boss."

Zane trotted off and Jason looked me up and down and seemed content that I would be able to physically do the job. He spoke as he walked us over to a large stack of steel beams.

"You know he pays double if you take the legal route, plus health benefits."

"I'm not sure about staying in town, just yet. I have to talk to my brother and see if he wants to or not," I answered.

"How old is he?"

"Twelve."

"That's a great age. I remember when my kid brother was twelve. He was always so curious about everything and obsessed with comic books." Jason said, his face breaking out in a warm, reminiscing smile.

"River hasn't gotten into comic books.

He prefers non-fiction books. He's a little weird but I love him anyway," I said, flashing a smile and chuckling.

River was very different to most twelve year old boys, but that was what I loved about him. He didn't care that he was smart. To him, that was who he was. If he went to school, when he went, people would see him as a nerd and pick on him. I didn't want that for him. I wanted him to feel comfortable with himself and that included his brilliant mind.

"He sounds like a smart kid. This world needs more smarts in it. Have you ever worked with steel before?"

"I have, same as cement."

I had worked at a good variety of construction sites. From building pools to commercial to residential, I could do it all. I just couldn't use the main equipment that required a certificate or a license.

"Good, that's what our primary mediums are. With this being a hotel and resort we have to follow commercial building codes. So steel and cement. Right now, we are working on the rebar forms for the underground parking structure. Then we'll pour the cement and form it. Do you have any licenses?"

"No. I've wanted to get a few for different equipment, but we don't tend to stick around in the same town long enough."

"Gaithersburg is a smallish town, but it's a good one. Despite what you may think, the construction workers in town do have enough work to keep them busy all year. I run the construction company and Zane controls the hires outside of my company. If you do a good job and stick around town, I would be happy to add you to my company once this project is done. We get a lot of work for the different cities, from homes to commercial. Hell, we even have a waitlist for pools. It's good money, but I do expect my guys to work hard and not disappear on me."

"I'll keep it in mind. Like I said, I'm not sure we'll end up staying that long."

I was surprised that he was offering me a job. He didn't know me. He didn't know what I was capable of. Yet, he was willing to offer me a job if I did good enough work for him.

I had no idea what it was about the people in this town, but they didn't act like I expected they would. I was waiting for them to demand something in return for their kindness, but so far, nothing had been asked of me.

I did need to talk to River and see how he felt. If he wanted to stay here and try to make a life, then I would do that for him. I would try and get the money for our own place saved up. I would get him in school and I would make sure he had a bright future ahead of him.

I knew I was the adult and I could just tell River that we were going to stay here, but I believed he had a right to have an opinion about the major decisions in his life. Choosing where to live was a major decision and he had a right to voice his opinions.

"Hopefully, you do. It's a nice town. Don't let the few bad apples push you away. We have to bring this stack of rebar into the hole for the steel workers."

I gave a nod and helped to carry the rebar over to the pit. There was a large pile and I knew based on the size of the hole, we would be using a hundred times the amount to make sure the structure was sound.

"Do you have family besides your brother?" I asked on our fourth round.

"No. My parents died a decade ago. It was just us."

"Was?" I was getting a bad feeling in the pit of my stomach that maybe his brother was dead. In which case, I felt like a jerk for bringing it up.

"My brother, Clay, was kidnapped when he was fourteen. Six years ago. The police looked everywhere, but he was never found. They suspected he was grabbed by human traffickers and could have been sent anywhere in the Country. I have a private investigator looking into his disappearance. He's been doing it for six years, now. But so far, nothing."

"I'm so sorry. I couldn't imagine going through that. To still be going through it after six years. I don't think I would be strong enough to handle the unknown of it."

I couldn't imagine losing River like that. To not know for six years if he was alive or dead. To not know if I was rooting for alive or dead. As terrible as it sounded, there were things worse than death. I wouldn't want River to be suffering and in pain for six years. either, if it could have been over for him. I wouldn't want him to be dead, but the thought of him being in horrible pain for years would be worse for him. Knowing that Jason was going through all of that and still working, still able to keep himself together, well, he earned a great deal of respect.

"It's hard, there are a lot of nights where I sit up and beg for my phone to ring and it be him on the other end. I haven't changed my phone number or moved so he always knows where I am or how to get a hold of me. Even his room is the exact same. The police stopped looking into it. They all say that he's dead. But without a body, I refuse to believe it. He wasn't book smart, and I say that with love. But he was street smart. He knew how to survive and there's a good chance he has survived and is out there somewhere."

"I believe that kids are resilient and know how to survive horrible situations, better than adults do. I'm sure one day you will find him." I didn't know if that would be true, but for his sake, and for his brother's sake, I hoped it would come true.

Jason seemed like a good man. I hadn't known him for very long, minutes really, but he had a presence about him. He came across as a good man that cared about people. I didn't feel any negative vibes from him. I was a firm believer in listening to your gut and what your first impressions are of someone.

My gut was telling me that Jason was a good man.

I could tell he was in need of a change of topic so I switched to something lighter as we worked. The day was starting out well and I hoped it would continue.

# CHAPTER NINE

Sol

IT WAS JUST after seven at night when River and I walked into the motel room.

He had spent the day with Max and he had talked the whole way home about everything that Max had taught him. I suspected that Max had one hell of a life before he was homeless, because he seemed to know a lot about different things.

I had been able to make eighty dollars today at work and despite trying to give half to Max, he refused to take it. The added amount allowed me to get River a Happy Meal, a treat that, normally, he only got on his birthday or Christmas Eve.

River went over to his bed and bounced down onto it with a smile as he opened the Happy Meal box.

"How was work?" he asked as I locked the door before sitting down across from him and pulling out my cheeseburger.

"It was good. We are working on the underground parking structure for the resort."

"Wow, it must be a big job."

"It is, actually. The underground parking is going to be four floors and then the resort is supposed to be sixteen floors. It's going to have hotel rooms, but also a pool with a manmade sand beach entrance to it. There's going to be shops and spas that will make up the first five floors. It'll be a year or longer before it's finished."

"What kind of shops?"

"I don't know. It's a resort, so there'll be retail shops and restaurants, I would imagine. There's going to be at least two coffee shops to be able to handle that amount of guests. People all over the construction site are talking about it and they can't wait to see the final project. It's supposed to bring in a lot of money to the owner, Zane, who will give some back to the town to build more affordable housing. It'll also create some jobs for people. It looks like this town might be expanding.”

I was trying to get an idea for how River was feeling about this town. The trick was, he did a lot better if you flat out asked him versus tiptoeing around. I just wasn't sure if he wanted me to ask.

“It's sounds like the town will benefit from the resort, too, that's nice. There is a lot of land that all belongs to the town that is left undeveloped because no one has the funds or the interest in building. I get the feeling that the town likes being smaller and doesn't want the expansion. After all, with expansion of new stores, it can reduce the profits of the smaller stores that have always been here. Evolution isn't just for people, though, but cities as well. If the town doesn't evolve, then they risk it being destroyed when the older population dies out and the younger population leaves for a more affluent city."

"Where did you learn all of that?" I asked, flashing him a warm smile.

"Max was teaching me about political science and economic structures today. It sounded interesting and opened my mind to a lot of different possibilities in the future. Do you like this town?"

"My boss, Zane, he said, if I wanted to, I could go on paper and be legal. I would make twice the amount I would in cash and I would even get health benefits. That would be nice in case you get sick again. The foreman, Jason, he even said if I do a good job on this project he would hire me for his construction site where I could have work all year around. Would you be open to the idea of staying here?"

"In this motel?" River asked, slightly

confused.

River was very smart, but sometimes he didn't understand exactly what you meant. I suspected it had to do with his intelligence, that he missed some social queues, and every now and then he doesn't register sarcasm. It never bothered me and I always explained to him what was said.

"In this town. We would have to stay in the motel until I was able to afford a place for us, and find one, but you could go to school. There's one just ten minutes from here. We could start to build a life together here, if you wanted to."

"I could go to school?" River asked, hopefully.

And just like that, I knew what his answer would be. He didn't care where we lived as long as he got to go to school, and

I couldn't blame him. His brain had been starving for four years now and it wanted to eat.

He needed to be in school.

He needed to be socialized, but he needed the chance to learn everything his mind wanted. I truly believed that he had the intelligence and heart to change this world and I was not doing him or this world any good by keeping him out of school. It would be a risk staying here, but it was a risk I had to take.

For River.

"You could, yes. I could go down tomorrow to get the paperwork and see what we need to do to get you enrolled. I know it's only been three weeks since it started, so you wouldn't be too far behind."

I also had no idea what grade he would

be in. At twelve, he could be in either grade six or seven. He was smart, so I wasn't worried about him not being able to catch up. I was worried about the basic curriculum that he would have missed over the past four years. There would be a lot he didn't know that everyone else would. However, I knew he would catch up. If there was one thing that River loved to do, it was to learn.

"Yes, please. If I can go to school, I vote we stay."

"Then we stay. I'll go tomorrow morning on my way to work to find out what we need to do. Maybe you can ask Max what you might need to know for grade six."

Max might have an idea. He seemed like a smart man himself. I had no idea why he was homeless, but it didn't seem like he had a mental disorder. I had never seen him drink or do drugs, either. He could be a veteran. He wouldn't be the first Vet that we had come across during our travels. They were always great with River and I tended to trust them the most to protect River while I was working.

"Okay, I'll ask him. This is exciting! I'll get to go to school and learn so much. Imagine how big the library will be," River said, a huge smile plastered across his face.

"I bet it's going to be pretty awesome," I agreed, flashing him a warm smile.

I wasn't sure how well staying would go, but it was a risk I had to take.

Even if I ended up being arrested if the truth came out.

It would be worth it to ensure that River got to experience life as a child. That was all that I cared about and it was damned time I started to build a life for him.

A proper life.

Hopefully, it wouldn't come back to bite me in the ass.

# CHAPTER TEN

Isaiah

IT HAD BEEN six days since I had last seen Sol and River at my office.

Over the course of the week, I had been busy with work. Travis and I had started to get a plan together for what we wanted the group home to be. I had hoped our boss would be taking some control over it, but he said it would be for the task force and it rested on our shoulders. I wasn't too happy about that because it was going to be a huge undertaking and it would have been nice to have some help from an executive position.

He had been working for Social Services for twenty years. He had a great deal of experience that we could have tapped into. Unfortunately, he was nearing the end of his employment and only had months until he retired. So, I guess I could understand him not wanting to invest any time in a project that could potentially derail his retirement for another year or so.

It also meant in the middle of all of this, I would have to deal with a new director that could make getting a group home started more difficult. It was just one more thing that was up in the air and it was not doing my nerves any favors.

I knocked on the motel room door once I arrived and, after a moment, the door opened to reveal a freshly showered Sol. He looked even better with his long, dark hair down around his shoulders and not pulled back in a braid. He gave me a small smile as he stepped back and spoke.

"Isaiah."

"Good afternoon, Sol. How are you doing?" I asked, being friendly but not overly so.

I knew that the majority of my clients weren't happy about seeing me. I was normally brought in because someone was questioning their ability to care for their child and that was never taken in a good light.

"Is this going to take long? River has homework," he asked in a tight voice and I could tell something was bothering him.

Something more than my presence.

"Not long at all. Where is River?"

"He just got out of the shower," Sol answered as he leaned against the top of the dresser that was set across from the beds.

"Were you able to find stable work, yet?"

I figured I might as well get started on what I needed to ask him while we waited for River to finish up from the shower.

"Zane put me on the books for the construction site. I get a paycheck every two weeks. He's going to pay me half in cash every day until my first pay comes in to help supplement until then."

"That's really good, Sol. Zane is a great

guy and the resort is going to bring in a lot of new jobs. People in town keep hoping he will run for mayor, but he doesn't seem to have the interest in it."

It really was too bad that Zane wasn't interested in being mayor. At least, not yet. He would have been a great man for the job. He would have made sure everyone that was lower than the rich were taken care of. He would make sure that there was equality within the town and the homeless were taken care of. He was also spearheading a very large project that would bring revenue into the town and create jobs.

Zane's resort was going to be amazing for the town and I was very thankful that the Mayor was happy with it and didn't try to stop the town from growing. Though, he would be receiving a lot of revenue himself from the taxes.

"He seems like a good guy," Sol said in a tight voice.

"Have you been able to look for a permanent place for you and River, yet? I know it's only been a week and there isn't much available in town, currently."

With a town this size, it normally took a bit before you would be able to find an apartment. They didn't often go up on the market and when they did, it was because the tenant was able to get their own home or they were moving out of town. It made it a bit difficult for new people in town to find a place.

"Not yet. We have the room for another week."

I gave a nod just as the bathroom door opened and I saw River come out. To my surprise, though, he had a four day old bruise to his right cheek. Instantly, my guard went up and my mind naturally went to assuming that it came from Sol.

"I need to speak with him alone. Please go and wait outside," I said to Sol without a single ounce of friendliness to my voice.

He didn't seem surprised at all and he just gave a warm wink to River before he headed out of the room. I turned and gave River my full attention as he went and sat down on his bed. I went over to him and sat down. This was not the first time I'd had to have this conversation with someone and I was hoping to never have it again.

"River, can I ask you about that bruise on your cheek?" I started with a calm voice.

"Yes," River answered as he opened his Math textbook.

"Did Sol hit you?"

River looked up at me before he spoke. "That's a very stereotypical assumption. Because we are Native, therefore, we must have anger issues? Sol has never raised a single hand to me. He doesn't even yell at me. My brother is above caveman-like traits that society has depicted as an acceptable and expected characteristic of an alpha male."

"Why do I get the feeling that one of the kids at your new school is not above their caveman-like traits?" I said, relaxing now.

This kid was far too smart for his own good and I knew the kids at the only public school in town could be a bit rough around the edges. River spoke very intelligently and that could come across as someone being a know-it-all.

"I don't know why you feel that way. But yes, a neanderthal at school did not appreciate me correcting their grammar. He said I had tooken his seat. Tooken is not a word. He didn't like me correcting him that it was *taken*."

"Can I ask you, River, do you ever feel like you don't understand some social situations or even sarcasm?"

River was a very smart boy and I would be speaking with Sol about him doing an IQ test, but I was getting the feeling that there was more to River's intelligence.

"People are hard. Books are easy," River answered.

"People can be very hard to understand, I completely agree with you. Books don't talk back or have feelings. You don't have to try and understand what they aren't saying. Books are very straightforward. How are you liking your school?"

"It's okay. I haven't been to one in a very long time. The work is easy, and my teacher seems nice. I don't really like recess or gym."

"I don't blame you about the gym part, but why don't you like recess? You don't like being able to run around and have fun?"

"Reading is fun. At recess, everyone just runs around with their friends. I don't really belong anywhere, yet. Sol said it would take time, but I would find my group of friends," River said with a small shrug.

"Being the new kid in school is never easy. Especially in a small town like this. Most of the kids have been in the same class since kindergarten so you are trying to fit into a group that has an impressive history. But Sol is right, you will find your group of friends. You will find people that you can connect with. Social situations are hard, but you can learn how to handle them."

River would fit in, but he would fit in better at the private school. I was convinced of that. I really hoped I would be able to pull some strings and get River in. He would excel much better with having the more advanced classes, but they would have their own occupational therapist that could help guide River through the confusing social situations.

"I guess," River said, and I could tell he wasn't that convinced about it.

"Is there anything you want to talk about? Are you feeling stressed or worried about staying in town?"

"No," River simply said, before he turned his attention back to his Math textbook.

"Okay, I am going to go and speak with your brother. You have a good day, River," I said, warmly.

"You, too," River said, keeping his gaze down on his homework.

I headed out to see Sol leaning against the brick wall with his arms crossed over his chest. I could tell he was angry, but I wasn't certain how angry at the situation he was, versus the bruise on River's face. I didn't speak until I went and stood across from him.

"I'm sorry if me needing to speak with River alone upset you. But please understand, Sol, speaking with him alone was not a reflection of my opinion of you.

My job is to protect children. Children that have been hurt by those that are supposed to protect them the most. There are no fairy tales in my world. The children I am responsible for can't afford for me to believe in them."

I really hoped he would understand where I was coming from. I didn't want him to see me as the enemy, because I wasn't. I hated it when my client's parents saw me as the boogie monster coming to steal their children. For some reason, though, I desperately wanted Sol to know that I wasn't that person. I wasn't someone he had to fear or push away.

I wanted to know more about him and River. I hoped that maybe once all of this was over and done with we could be friends. He seemed like a nice person, even if he was always on edge when I was around.

"I'm not mad at you. I understand why you had to do it and I have nothing to hide. I've never raised a hand to him and I never would. I would lay my life down to protect him. I'm upset because all River has ever wanted since we left home was to go to school and when he finally does, it's hell for him. I knew he would have problems connecting with people, but I thought he would find at least one person in his class to be friends with."

I could hear his frustration, but I could also hear the self-hate in his voice. He was angry with himself for not being able to fix River's situation.

He was a good brother.

It was refreshing to see.

"There is a private school on the outskirts of town. There are a handful of full scholarships that they give out each year. They are very select, however, I think we could get River one of those scholarships," I started.

"What? How?" Sol asked, surprised.

"With your permission, I would like for River to get his IQ tested. I have a feeling he is a genius and, if it does come back that he is, they'll be more than happy to give him a scholarship."

I was hoping that Sol would agree to it, because I truly believed it would be best for River. He would be able to get the education that he needed, that he deserved, at a level that wasn't too easy or boring, one that was tailored to him alone, but also the help he needed for social situations. The private school had a lot of great clubs and even had a robotics lab. It was a dream come true for a genius student and I knew River would flourish there.

I could see the surprise within Sol's eyes and it was clear he was not used to having people help him out, at least people in authority, anyway. He seemed genuinely touched by my offer.

A good sign.

"Okay, how do we get his IQ tested?"

"He can do it at the school. It's free for children and you'll get the results back within hours. I can set it up for you, if you'd like," I offered.

"Thank you, I would appreciate that. He deserves to know what his IQ is, what his mind is capable of. It doesn't matter to me, but he needs to know. He has some quirks that I've always just accepted as a part of who he is, but I know he's not typical. He doesn't understand a lot of social situations and he doesn't seem to connect to people his age. He's better with adults. Adults tend to know better than to poke fun at him for what he misses in conversations."

"He could have a disorder. It wouldn't be uncommon for people with a high IQ to have a low emotional quota, but that can be learned and built up over time and practice. You have done a good job with him, Sol. He's a gifted and nice young man. With being in a proper school they will have professionals there that can take him the rest of the way," I said, flashing him a warm smile.

I wasn't about to let Sol believe he had failed River in any way. He was doing very good for River, given their circumstances. It wasn't easy to raise a child at his young age.

He was only nineteen.

He should be in school himself, and dating.

He should be living a carefree life and yet, he was working full-time and raising his twelve year old brother. Sol was a good man and he deserved a great deal of credit.

"Thank you, was there anything else you needed from me?"

"No, everything was good today. I'll be back next week and I'll let you know about a time for the IQ test," I said, and flashed him a friendly smile.

"Thanks," Sol said with a nod, and I knew we were done.

I said a quick goodbye before I made my way down the street and back to my office. This check in had gone well and I hoped that, soon, Sol and River would have their own place and be back on their feet.

# CHAPTER ELEVEN

Sol

MY FEET REFUSED to stay in one spot. I had walked up and down the short hallway easily a hundred times, now. I don't know why I was so nervous. It wasn't me writing the IQ test.

I hadn't told River about it until this morning. When Isaiah had said he would be able to get River in for an IQ test, I wanted to believe him, but I wasn't too sure. I didn't want to tell him about it until I knew for certain, because I knew he would have been excited to take it.

I wasn't too sure how well he would do. I didn't know what was on an IQ test and I knew there were a few areas of River's education that were lacking compared to others his age. We didn't really cover science or social studies while we were living on the streets.

I tried to get him to learn as much as he could. We were always going to the library for him to read different books and I made sure he read a good variety of non-fiction books to help him. It wasn't the same as being in school, though, with a teacher there to guide you.

When I told River this morning, he was very excited. I honestly hadn't seen him that happy in a very long time. School had been hard for him for the past two weeks. River was still not making friends and the other kids in his class were picking on him. They hadn't escalated to bullying, but I knew it would be coming soon if he didn't get out of that class, out of that school.

I prayed with everything in me that he would be able to do well on the IQ test and they would offer him a scholarship to the private school. It had been two hours and I had no idea how much longer this would go on for. I didn't know how long a normal IQ test would take, or if there was even a time limit on it. Finally, after another ten minutes the Headmistress came out of the room with River right behind her.

"Thank you, River. You can have a seat

just right here," Headmistress Susan said.

I wasn't sure why River had to wait, but she obviously wanted to talk to me, and that made my nerves skyrocket.

"I just need a moment of your time Mr. Lockheart," she said.

It wasn't my real last name, but it was a common Native American last name and should make things harder for anyone to try and find our history. I gave a nod and gave River a wink as I walked by him and into the room. Headmistress Susan spoke as she closed the door.

"Please, take a seat."

"Is everything okay?" I asked as I went and slid into a chair.

"Everything is more than okay. I wanted to discuss River's IQ test with you. We spoke with River and he informed us that he hasn't been in school steadily so we gave him an IQ test that was not focused around what he would have learned in school. We gave him one that would require his mind to figure out puzzles and different number sequences. Typically, this IQ test can take thirty minutes... however, River was able to get through it in ten. We've been here for so long because we have been giving him different IQ tests to try and gauge his IQ level. The average IQ level for a twelve year old is one hundred and eight. River's rough IQ level is one hundred and sixty."

"I'm sorry, what?" I asked, shocked.

I knew River would have a higher IQ, but I didn't think it would be that high. That seemed way too high for someone his age. I had no idea what the normal adult IQ level was, but even that seemed too high.

"Your brother is a genius. A child prodigy. He's very good with math and number sequences. He would do very well with coding and engineering. He speaks very well, but with an IQ that high we were concerned about his social skills. Our occupational therapist, Mr. Shew, spoke with River briefly and he suspects that River hits the autism spectrum, but on the high end. He described it as just kissing the spectrum so he needs a bit of work with handling and understanding social situations, but he isn't so far on the spectrum where it would be a detriment to his social development and ability to make friends."

I didn't know what to say. All of this was a lot of news coming at me. I knew what autism was, but from what I knew they could barely speak and they were often child-like.

River wasn't like that at all.

"I'm sorry, I just... I don't even know what that is. I know what autism is, but River isn't like any of the descriptions that I've heard," I said as I tried to catch up.

"That's okay, this is all going to be confusing and shocking to the both of you. Autism has two types, low end, which is what most people think of when they hear the word autism. However, there is also a high end functioning level and that is people that are geniuses who have difficulties with social situations. They also tend to speak later on in life than your average child. Where most children are speaking by eighteen months, children with high end autism might not speak until they are three. They tend to relate and interact better with adults. They tend to have little quirks, too. Have you noticed that River doesn't like the feel of certain fabrics or maybe he gets upset when a routine is disrupted?"

I had noticed a few things over the years, especially in the past four years with us being homeless. I hadn't read too much into it, though. I just figured it was his way of coping with the frequently moving.

River liked having a routine and I tried my best to keep it the same, no matter what town we were living in. He went to bed at the same time, woke up at the same time, and ate at the same time. Every other night was bath night, no matter where we did it. I couldn't keep everything the same, it just depended on where I was working, but I did try. River never cared for the feel of wool, not that I could blame him.

He had quirks, but didn't we all?

"I've always tried to keep his routine the same, but he gets unsettled if it deviates. I've always just kinda worked around him. What does this mean for River?" That was all I cared about.

"Nothing. He is still going to have an amazing life. It just lets us know that we have to work with him on his social skills, which can be learned. I would love to offer River a full scholarship," she said, and flashed me a warm smile.

"Really?" I knew Isaiah had said that River might be able to get a full scholarship, but I hadn't really believed him. I'd been trying to figure out what to say to River about why he couldn't go here. I would never be able to afford the tuition to a place like this.

"Yes, I have the paperwork here. I just need your signature in a couple of spots. The scholarship covers tuition, textbooks, lab fees, field trips, and any extra curricular fees that River would like to be a part of. We have a robotics team that I think he would love. This year, they are going to build a fighting robot and compete with it. The only thing it doesn't cover is the cost of the uniforms. We get them through a local shop. I have a pamphlet here for you," she said as she pushed the pamphlet over to me.

A quick look told me it was three hundred dollars for a single uniform outfit and River would need at least two of them. I had no idea how I was going to come up with the money. Or rather I did, but it was the last thing I wanted to do.

"Now, I just need you to sign a few pieces of paper and it will get everything set in motion. I will reach out to his current school and get whatever they have on file for him, which I don't expect is much with how short he's been there. He could start tomorrow morning," she said.

"That fast, wow. Um, what about the difference in schooling? There is a lot he doesn't know now that everyone else does. Won't that be an issue for him here?"

"He will have a tutor, which is covered under the scholarship. The tutor will make sure he is all caught up. River will work with his tutor every day to make sure he doesn't get left behind. He's in grade six at the current school but I would recommend that you consider having him start here in grade seven. He won't be the only twelve year old in the class and I think he would benefit from the academic challenge before moving on to high school. He does have quite a bit he would need to catch up on, socially speaking, and it would give him a bit of time to adjust to being in a school like this before his class work gets harder with being in the senior grades."

I wasn't sure about any of this. I didn't graduate high school. I barely made it through grade school with having to work to support the household. I only got one year in high school before we had to go on the run from Phillip. This was way out of my league and I had no idea what to do about any of this.

"I don't know much about any of this. I have worked most of my life and school wasn't something that came first. If you think having him in grade seven would be better for him, then that's fine with me. I don't want him feeling overwhelmed or stupid if he can't handle it, though."

"And that is the last thing I want as well. His intellect level is why I think he would thrive with being in grade seven, as he says the work now is too easy and boring, which we find tends to turn children off because they aren't engaged enough, and like I said, it gives us a couple of year to work with him on his social skills, as well."

"Okay, if you think it's best, then I'm okay with it."

I had no idea what would be best for River and if the Headmistress, a teacher, was recommending something different then I was going to go with her on it. She was a professional and knew what was best.

We spent the next fifteen minutes going over all of the paperwork and part of me felt like an idiot because I didn't understand half of it. This was why I worked with my hands. Building was easy, you followed the plan and at the end of it you had accomplished something. There wasn't much critical thinking involved. She was patient, though, I had to give her that much. She didn't get annoyed when I asked her any questions.

"Perfect, I will get these filed into our system and let River's teacher know he will be joining her tomorrow. He will need his uniform, but Randal, the shop owner, always has items in stock. I am also giving these to River to use for his school work. An iPad and a laptop. He can have them in class and take them home so he can continue to do his homework with them. They are his to keep and any software that he needs for any extracurriculars can be added to them. His teacher, Mrs. David, will have his textbooks for him and everything he needs tomorrow morning."

"That's it? I don't have to do anything else for him?"

"Nope, that's it. I am very excited and happy to have River joining us. I think he's going to love being here," she said, flashing me a warm smile.

"I think so, too. Thank you so much," I said as I held my hand out to her.

She easily took it as we both stood. "Thank you for bringing him in. He's got one hell of a future ahead of him."

We said goodbye and I strolled out to see River sitting there, waiting patiently. I gave him a warm smile and a nod so we could head out. I waited to talk until we hit the sidewalk and were on our way back to the motel.

"Well, you are officially enrolled there. You even got a new laptop and iPad to use for your school work," I said, a proud smile splitting my face.

"Shut up! Are you serious?" River asked, and his eyes lit up with the biggest smile I had ever seen crossing his features.

"Dead serious. Tomorrow, we will head out and get you your uniform and then I'll drop you off at school. When we get back to the motel, you should look over the iPad and laptop to make sure you know how to use it all."

I hoped he would be able to figure it out, because I had no idea how any of that stuff worked.

I didn't even know how to drive.

That was something I would need to figure out with us staying here. I would need to learn how to drive and get my driver's license so I could travel to different towns for work.

"That is so cool. The school has a robotics lab, they build actual robotics, how insane is that?" River asked, full of excitement now.

"Very insane. You think you'll join the club?"

"I can?" River asked, hopeful.

"Of course you can. The scholarship covers everything. You can join any club you want. All you have to do is let me know your schedule so I can make sure I pick you up."

"Deal," River easily agreed.

I listened to River talk about the school the whole way back to the motel. Once there, he was instantly going onto the iPad and exploring it. I would have to go out tonight to make the money for his uniforms, but it would be worth it. This was River's future and I was not going to jeopardize it for anything.

# CHAPTER TWELVE

Sol

IT WAS NEARING three in the morning and I had finally made enough for River's uniforms. I was exhausted and I needed a shower, but even then I didn't think I would ever feel clean.

I hated doing this.

I hated selling my body to these disgusting men, but it was the only way I would be able to afford River's uniforms.

I was making my way back to the motel when there were suddenly hands on my arms dragging me into the side alley. I fought to get them off, but there was more than one set of hands.

"Let's teach this little faggot a lesson," a foreign male voice said.

Before I even had the chance to defend myself, I was being hit. I tried to fight them off, but there were three of them and I was never much of a fighter. It wasn't long before I was on the ground and curling up into a tight ball to try and protect my body. Their blows kept coming and I had no idea if they were ever going to stop. I had been in a fight before, it wasn't uncommon with being homeless, and the end result was usually the same for me.

I didn't know how long it had been, but eventually their blows stopped and I heard them walk away. The whole world was spinning, but nothing hurt. I knew that wouldn't last long, that it was just my body in shock, and once it wore off I would be feeling it all.

I moved my hand down to make sure the money I had was still there. I had tucked it into my boot, because then I wouldn't have to worry about someone trying to grab it from my pocket. Plus, it wasn't like I got naked around my Johns. I just needed to lower my pants enough. A wave of relief hit me when I felt the money was still there. I had gotten jumped, but at least I hadn't lost the seven hundred dollars I had made tonight.

I forced my body to move. I needed to get going and be back at the motel before the shock wore off and the pain kicked in. I knew come morning I would be hurting, but I would need to lie about any bruises. I wasn't about to let River's first day in his new school be tainted.

I forced my body to move toward the motel and once I arrived, I very quietly slid inside. I instantly saw River sleeping on his bed with his backpack already set for tomorrow and the sight made me smile.

Slowly, I made my way into the bathroom. I needed a shower and I needed to see the damage done. I didn't want to know, but I had to. Seeing my reflection only confirmed what I suspected. I wouldn't be able to lie about it. I was already getting bruises around my left eye. My lip was split and there was blood coming from my nose.

There was no hiding that I had been in a fight.

Letting out a small sigh, I had no choice but to get into the shower. I had to be up in under three hours to make sure that River was up, fed, and ready to go for the uniform shop that opened at seven.

I then had a long day at work.

I groaned at that thought.

I knew Zane would let me off with being injured, but I couldn't afford the missed work. We needed every cent we could get. This wouldn't be the first time I worked injured and it wouldn't be the last.

River was all that mattered and there was nothing that was going to ruin his day tomorrow.

# CHAPTER THIRTEEN

Isaiah

IT HAD BEEN a month since I first started to see Sol and River.

I never would have thought that I would feel this way about a client, and yet, I was.

I liked Sol.

I liked him far more than I should as a caseworker.

I wasn't supposed to like him in that way. I was supposed to keep everything professional, but it was getting harder and harder to keep it that way.

When I went and saw him for his second check in, he had bruises all over his face and I suspected there were more underneath his clothes. I had asked him when we were alone what had happened, but he refused to talk about it. Someone had jumped him, or multiple people had, I was sure of it. I wanted him to open up to me and report it to the police, but he wasn't budging. I had even tried asking River, but he said it was a work accident. He wasn't lying, but I also knew it wasn't the whole truth.

It was just what Sol had told his brother.

I was allowing my personal feelings to

get in the way of my professional interactions with Sol and I knew it. I had always been able to keep my feelings out of my work. Hell, I had never had feelings or felt attracted to one of my clients before.

I kept telling myself that it was Sol's eyes. They were breathtaking and unique, and that had to be the reason why I couldn't get him out of my mind. I knew I was fooling myself, though, because it wasn't just his eyes.

I wanted to spend more time with him.

I found myself coming up with conversations to start with him during our weekly check ins just to spend more time with him. I would walk by the construction site, even though it was further out of my way, with the hope of seeing him and getting that chance to speak with him outside of a professional manner. So far, all I had been able to accomplish was a few glances of him as he worked hard.

I was being pathetic, lingering around hoping to catch a passing glance at a boy that I liked.

It was pathetic and it had to stop.

I had to stop.

That is what brought me to the bar tonight. I couldn't keep doing it. I couldn't keep going that way.

I was going to finally rip the bandaid off and have sex.

I was far too old to be a virgin and I just needed to finally do it. I was too old to believe in my first time being special. My time to lose my virginity to a man that I loved had long passed. The problem was, I had no idea how to do that.

I had no idea how to hit on someone, or pick someone up in a bar. I had never done that before. The other man always started the few relationships that I'd had. They ended by him, too. I never had to try and pick someone up in a bar. I'd never held an interest in it. I still didn't, truth be told, but it seemed like the only way I was going to be able to move on was to be with someone.

"Can I buy you a drink?"a male voice said right next to me and it snapped me out of my thoughts.

I instantly turned to look at the man, I was surprised to see him so close to me and I hadn't noticed.

"Um... sure," I said.

He was a good looking man. He had light brown hair that was on the shorter side, but it wasn't too short. There was enough there that I could run my hands through it and make it messy. His eyes were blue, but they were nothing compared to Sol's eyes. Compared to the blue of Sol's eyes, this man's eyes looked dull and lifeless. He was well built, but unlike Sol, his body's muscles came from the gym and not hard, manual labor.

It wasn't lost on me that I kept comparing this stranger to Sol.

I needed to get Sol out of my system. It was the only way that I would be able to maintain professionalism with him.

The man gave a nod to the bartender and held up two fingers to indicate his order before he sat down beside me.

"I'm James."

"Isaiah," I said, slightly awkwardly.

"I haven't seen you here before. You new in town?"

I was pretty much never here. When I first moved to town, I would go down to the gay bar in a neighboring town. Gaithersburg was starting to become more progressive and forward thinking, but they were not at the level of having a gay bar. After being in town for a year, I stopped going there because everyone seemed to only be interested in having meaningless sex.

There were a few different gay bars or clubs within an hour of Gaithersburg, but everyone knew this bar was where you went if you wanted a one-night stand.

It was why I came here tonight.

"No, I just don't go out very often," I answered as our drinks arrived.

"That's a shame. Someone that looks as good as you should never be kept locked inside," he said, flashing me a flirty smirk.

He was using a pick up line that I was certain he had probably used over a hundred times already. I knew he didn't truly mean it, because someone like him did not tend to go for someone like me.

I was chubby, smart, and awkward.

This man was good looking and dressed to impress.

He was most likely an office executive. Men like him didn't go for men like me. That is, unless given next to no choice.

The bar tonight wasn't very busy on account it was a Wednesday and most of the people in here were already paring off. James only had two choices. Either go home and accept that he didn't get to have sex tonight, or to go with me. Apparently, going with me was the better option for him.

I should have been insulted by that, and there was a part of me that was. A big part of me. At the same time, though, I was here for the exact same reason. I was here to have sex and for it to be with some random stranger, to finally get it over and done with. I didn't have any right to be insulted when I was here for the exact same reason as him.

To have meaningless sex.

"I work a lot," I said, not really sure how to respond to him.

It wasn't that I didn't know how to be social. I had gotten a lot of practice with my job. Still, I was a bit awkward outside of work. It was a result of growing up in a cult like the FLDS. We were not allowed to interact with outsiders so we didn't know how to be social around *normal* people.

I had worked hard on it when I was

younger, when I first got out. It was overwhelming, though, but I had pushed through it because I knew it was vital to my professional life. I had to be able to talk and interact with people, especially with wanting to be a social worker. I couldn't be awkward and unsure around children that were scared and needed help.

There was still this area of awkwardness when it came to dating, though. It was why I almost never dated, because I didn't know how.

"Me too. I'm an investor at an investment firm. What do you do?"

Of course he was an investor. I had a feeling he worked in some fancy corner office. There were a lot of executives that would come down to these places. They weren't able to be out and open with their jobs, so they would come to places like this when they needed to release some steam.

"Social worker."

"Oh, that's interesting. You must be buried under paperwork."

"There is a lot of it, yes."

Most people didn't want to talk about my job. I was a social worker and to most people it was one of the furthest jobs you could get from glamorous. I could understand that. I was a social worker and in society people viewed me as a thief that came in and stole children from happy homes.

James downed his drink before he spoke.

"Why don't we go into one of the backrooms?"

This bar was so infamous for random

hookups that they had back rooms with a bed in them to make it easier for people to have sex. They didn't take any money for it, so it was legal. They kept everything clean just like a hotel room.

Still, I never thought I would be losing my virginity in one.

I gave a shaky nod and James stood. I let out a small breath before I got up and followed him through the small crowd on the dance floor to the back room area. He went into the first available room and once I walked in, he closed the door.

The room itself wasn't anything fancy. It looked a lot like a rundown motel room that you would find on a side highway in the middle of nowhere. There was just a bed and a bedside lamp that sat on a very old looking nightstand. It wasn't a place you would want to lose your virginity in, that was for sure, and yet, here I was.

I was still standing here and about to go through with it.

I was going to lose my virginity in this room to a complete stranger.

I startled just slightly when I felt James' hands on my hips from behind me. He gave a dark chuckle as he started to kiss all along my neck.

"Someone is a bit jumpy. You're not nervous, are you?"

I would have been honest with him about being nervous had he not spoken the question in a teasing voice. He didn't care how I was feeling because he was only focused on his own desires. He was horny and needed to have sex. I was just the person he was able to pick up.

It was just that simple.

I knew he wanted to have sex, I could

feel him hard already. The problem was, I wasn't. I knew he hadn't really touched me yet, outside of holding my hips and pressing his lips to my neck, but I hadn't touched him, either.

Shouldn't I be feeling something?

Even though he hadn't really touched me, shouldn't I be turned on and feeling excited about what was to come?

When I had started dating other guys I would be excited and anxious to do things with them. I was never this nervous and, normally, I would be aroused before we even did anything.

I was so nervous right now I thought I might throw up from it.

James moved around me and started to kiss me.

I kissed him back, but I wasn't feeling it. He was dominant, if his kiss was anything to go by. He didn't give me much of a chance to adjust to his lips against my own before he was trying to shove his tongue into my mouth.

This was wrong.

All of this was wrong.

The room, the man, everything.

I couldn't do this.

No matter how badly I wanted to lose my virginity, I couldn't give it to this man.

I put my hands on his chest and pushed him back gently. I forced him to stop the kiss and I could see he was slightly annoyed by me taking control.

"I'm sorry, I can't do this. It's not you, it's me."

"What are you talking about? It's just sex, it's not a big deal. Fuck, I would think a guy like you would be happy when any man showed an interest in fucking you."

Wow, he was charming.

And that was only further proof as to why this was a bad idea.

I had been carrying around my virginity all of these years and he didn't deserve to have it.

"Go fuck yourself, James," I said, flashing him a friendly smile before I turned and strolled out of the room at a fast pace.

I was not going to allow a man like that to touch me.

I wanted to have sex, I wanted to lose my virginity, and I wanted to get Sol out of my head. However, I was not going to just give it to the first man that came across my path.

I wasn't going to allow any man to use me like that.

I would figure out how to forget about Sol and make sure my feelings stayed professional with him. I would do it without selling my soul or losing a piece of myself.

# CHAPTER FOURTEEN

Sol

I WAS EXHAUSTED. I had been working hard over the past two months at the construction site. I was grateful to be able to work on the site and, hopefully, have a job afterward. It was nice not having to stress about finding work.

I was still worried about money, though. I still had to pay for the motel every week, plus try and save up enough money for a place of our own. Thankfully, nothing had really come up in town within the past two months that was available to rent. Still, I wanted to have enough money saved up for first and last month's rent so when an apartment did become available, I would be able to put my name in the running for it. If I didn't have the funds, no landlord would pick us over someone who could put down the money required.

The result, though, was long hours at the construction site doing everything I could do to keep showing that I was a hard and dedicated worker. I was exhausted more times than not at the end of the day, but I knew it would all be worth it so River would have a proper place to live. I wanted River to have his own bedroom desperately and I was truly hoping I could make it happen soon.

River had been doing amazing at his new school. He no longer had any problems with the kids in his class. There was no bullying. The school had a zero tolerance for it and none of the children were going to risk being expelled. River had flourished under the new curriculum. He was in love with the robotics team and was often staying late to work on their fighting robot. Him staying late meant I could stay late and pull in some overtime to make extra money. It was going well, very well, and we were falling into a routine.

The school had sent River to speak with a professional that was able to evaluate River and he was able to determine that River was on the autism spectrum. He was on the high end of the spectrum and just kissing it, as the headmistress had suspected. It meant he would be able to navigate through life without too many difficulties.

He was working with the occupational therapist that worked at the school. She was amazing and would be able to help River learn how to react to certain social situations. The school was a Godsend and I was completely relieved to have decided to stay here.

I hadn't been too sure, at first, about staying in town, especially after Isaiah grabbed River. But it turned out to be a good decision, possibly one of the best decisions of my life, in fact.

Staying here meant we had been able to get River into a proper school, to get the education he needed. I was able to get a job that paid well and even had health benefits for River. Things were finally looking up for us and it seemed like we could actually build a real home here.

Today was Saturday and I had been at the site all day. We were set to have a check in with Isaiah in the next ten minutes and I needed to get back to the motel and make sure the room was clean.

River wasn't a messy kid, the opposite actually, but he could get lost in his mind and not realize how much time had gone by. He was often working away at his laptop on either homework or something for the robotics team. There were plenty of times when I'd come home from work and River had been working all day long and hadn't eaten anything. That was why I had made sure to set an alarm on the clock in the room to go off every three hours. That way, River would come up for air and eat something.

I walked into the motel room, but instead of seeing River sitting on his bed, there was no one.

River wasn't here.

I had to hold off on panicking, because there could be any number of reasons why River wasn't in the room. I walked over and looked in the bathroom, but just as I suspected, he wasn't in it.

On the bed sat his laptop and iPad, both turned off.

I went over to the small closet and opened the door. His school bag was sitting on the floor where he always left it. I grabbed his bag and looked inside to see his textbooks were all there as well. I put it back before looking all over the room.

Maybe he'd gone to the library, but if

he did there had to be a note somewhere to tell me. The problem was, there was nothing. No matter where I looked, I couldn't find a note telling me where he went. There was nothing to indicate that he had left or why.

I could feel the panic starting to build up in my chest.

River wasn't there.

I knew he was twelve and he could have just gone off with friends or to the library, but he always left a note. He knew he couldn't just wander off. He knew he had to let me know where he was going and he had to be with someone. If he wasn't with someone, he had to be in the motel room with the door locked at all times. There was no reason why he would be out there on his own. He should be in the room.

My mind couldn't stop thinking about all of the possibilities about what could have happened to River.

What if Phillip had found us and he was grabbed?

What if someone saw that River was alone and decided to grab him and he could now be anywhere all because I went to work on a Saturday?

I knew I was spinning out, that I had to try and calm down and get my thoughts in order, but I couldn't seem to get myself to stop and focus. I was too busy worrying about the worst case scenario.

I couldn't help it.

When I'd spent so long on the run, hiding and being scared that someone was going to discover who we truly were, it was natural for my mind to jump to that conclusion.

My spiraling out of control mind came to a screeching halt when there was a knock at the door. I looked up and saw that Isaiah was standing there in the open doorway. I could see the concern across his face and I knew I must look like a crazy person right now.

"Sol, what's wrong?" he asked, gently, as he made his way over to me cautiously. As if I was a wild animal and he thought I could strike him if he got too close.

"River. He's not here. He's supposed to be here."

The panicked tone to my voice sounded crazy when you heard my words. River was twelve. It really wasn't that big of a deal for him to be late or not show up.

To me, though, it was huge.

It was potentially the end of the world because my baby brother, the brother that I had been raising practically his whole life, was now missing and I had no idea where he was or what was happening to him.

Isaiah spoke calmly as he raised his hands up in a surrender position. "It's okay, take a breath and start at the beginning. Was River supposed to be here?"

I took a few deep breaths, or at least I tried to. I didn't realize that my whole body was shaking until right that moment. I needed to try and get my mind to focus so I could figure out where to start looking for River. I felt Isaiah place his hands on my biceps and then he gently guided me over to my bed, coaxing me to sit down on the edge of it. He bent down so he was eye level with me as he spoke.

"I need you to try and breathe for me, Sol. You are on the verge of hyperventilating. I need you to take a slow and deep breath. Can you do that for me, Honey?"

The warmth and calming sound in Isaiah's voice was helping to calm my nerves down. His voice always seemed to have an effect on me. It always made me feel warm and safe. It made no sense because he was still virtually a stranger to me. There was no reason for me to feel anything toward him and yet, I did.

It also wasn't lost on me that he referred to me as *Honey*.

To me, that was a term of endearment, but perhaps to him, in his line of work, it was a common thing for him to do. What wasn't helping was my panicking. That wasn't going to help me find River and that was all that mattered.

I closed my eyes and did what Isaiah said. I focused on my breathing and took some calming breaths. I used my breathing techniques that I used to when Phillip would come into my room. He didn't like it if I showed that I didn't want him. That ruined it for him and then he got angry. When he was angry, he made sure it hurt.

Thinking about Phillip made my breathing start to increase so I forced those thoughts from my mind and focused on the warmth that was coming from Isaiah's hands on my biceps.

I normally hated being touched by anyone that wasn't River, but for some reason feeling Isaiah's hands on my skin didn't make me want to throw up. They were warm and his heat seemed to seep into my skin. I could smell his cologne and it always reminded me of the woods. I had no idea what it was called, but it reminded me of being back home. We could always smell the woods from our house and it was my favorite scent.

As I focused my thoughts on Isaiah, I was able to get my breathing back to normal. I knew that was something I would have to reflect upon later, but right now was not the time.

I opened my eyes and Isaiah gave me a warm and kind smile.

"That's good. Now, can you tell me what happened?"

"There was some overtime available at work and Zane always offers it to me first. I went into work at eight. River was already up and was eating breakfast. I told him I would see him tonight at three and I reminded him that you would be coming by for your check in. He said he knew and rolled his eyes at me." I started, but I couldn't help the small smile at the memory of River rolling his eyes. He didn't tend to do it often, but when he did I never got mad. It was the most typical kid thing he ever did.

"I told him to lock up and I waited until I heard both locks before I went to work. When I came back, he wasn't here. The door was locked, but he wasn't here. He's always been here. And I know, technically, he should have a babysitter, but he doesn't leave the room."

Isaiah spoke, cutting me off before I could go any further. "River is twelve, he's not two. He's more than capable of being left alone for the day. You didn't leave him alone for the weekend or overnight. You didn't leave him standing on a street corner and tell him you would be back in ten minutes. He's twelve. He has everything he needs here. There's nothing wrong with that, Sol. Maybe he went to go and meet up with a friend?"

"No, he would have left a note. He knows he has to leave a note of where he is going, who he is going with, and when he is coming back. That's the rule and he never breaks the rules. Also, if he was going to meet up with a friend, he would have taken his laptop or iPad with him. He only has friends in the robotics team and they always work on some new code. They don't play sports or go shopping."

"Okay, maybe he went to the library for a book?"

"He's supposed to be here. He knows he can't be out there on his own, it's not safe for him to be out there alone."

"Why isn't it safe for him to be out there on his own, Sol?"

Shit.

I shouldn't have said that.

It wouldn't make sense for me to say that a twelve year old in a small town wouldn't be safe out on his own during broad daylight. I had to be more careful with what I said around Isaiah.

It wasn't about trust.

Part of me did trust him with the truth. Far too much of me trusted him when I barely knew anything about him. I wanted to tell him the truth. It would make this a lot easier.

I had to find River and if that meant I would have to tell Isaiah, eventually, about the truth to why I had River, then I would. Right now, though, I had to find River and he didn't need to know that story to help me find him.

"I have to find River." I spoke as I started to get up.

"I'll help you look for him. Let's go and speak with the manager at the front desk. He might have seen something," Isaiah offered.

I just gave a nod and we both headed out. We made the short walk to the front office and the second we walked in I instantly went over to the desk.

"Bobby, did you see River leave the room today?"

"Um, yeah. He left about two hours ago when your father showed up."

My stomach felt like it fell out of my body.

We didn't have a father.

Our father was gone and that meant whoever had River was a complete stranger.

A man that could potentially hurt him.

My worst nightmare was coming true and I had allowed it to happen.

I was at work when I should have been here with him, then he never would have been taken. I would have been there to protect him and stop this from happening.

This was my fault.

This was all my fault.

"We don't have a father."

"What did this man look like?" Isaiah immediately asked.

"Uh, he had short, blonde hair, green eyes. He was average height, average weight. He spoke with an accent, a southern drawl, and he had a scar through his left eyebrow."

Oh no.

Phillip.

Holy shit, it was Phillip.

This couldn't be happening.

No.

Out of all the people that could have taken River, he was the worst option. I had always felt like someone was watching us, following us around. It was why I made sure we moved so often. Why I made sure we traveled in all directions without creating a pattern. I made sure to cover our tracks as best as possible, even changing our names when we got to a new town. I made sure we were kept as hidden as possible.

"It's Phillip. Phillip Morris," I said as I ran my hands over my face.

"Who is that?" Isaiah asked.

"A very bad man. He'll hurt River. I don't know how he found us. We have to call the police."

It would make everything come out into the light and I knew I was going to lose River once this came out, but I didn't care about that.

I had to get to River.

I had to find River and make sure he was okay. Nothing else mattered but that. I would happily spend the rest of my life in a jail cell if it meant that River would be safe.

Dear God, please don't let Phillip get the chance to hurt my brother.

Don't let him take away River's innocence the way he stole mine.

# CHAPTER FIFTEEN

Isaiah

THE VERY LAST thing I expected today when I went for my check in with Sol was to discover that River was missing.

When he first told me that River wasn't there, I didn't think much of it. River was a twelve year old boy. It was natural for him to go out with friends during the day, especially on a weekend. It didn't seem like anything that would cause a person to be alarmed.

I knew Sol and River were close, but I didn't think they would be that close. Close to the point where Sol had to know where River was at all times. It seemed extreme, but now maybe there was a reason for it. There was more going on with Sol and River. There was so much more to their story, and whoever this Phillip Morris man was, he was a big part of it.

I knew it would be best to call the police. I knew that was what you did when a complete stranger has taken a child. You call the police and let them handle it. And yet, everything in me was screaming to not do it.

To go a different way.

I had no idea what Sol's story was, but

my gut was telling me he might not have had permission to take River. I knew that meant I should call the police even more, if Sol had kidnapped River. But I also knew that I had done the exact same thing with my sisters.

I had kidnapped them.

I had taken them across state lines and I knew what it felt like to live in fear of that truth being exposed. If Sol was in the same position, I wasn't about to turn him in, not when there was another option to getting River back.

"Bobby, did you happen to get a license plate or a look at his car?" I asked.

"It was a black Chevy pick up truck. It looked old, and I only saw the last three numbers, five, nine, zero."

"Thanks." I pulled out my cell phone and called the one person I knew would be able to help us.

"Damien. We have an emergency. A twelve year old boy. River. He's one of my charges. He's been kidnapped. A man named Phillip Morris came to the motel claiming to be his father and he took him. His brother, Sol, said they don't have a father and that Phillip is a bad man and will hurt River."

"Then call the police."

"That's not an option. We have a vehicle model and a partial plate. We're two hours behind."

I knew that Damien would run it. We were talking about a missing kid. There was no way he wasn't going to run the plate or the name. Besides, Damien had always had my back. Whenever I needed help, I would go to him and I knew he would be there for me. He was a good man that only cared about helping people.

"What is it?"

"Old black Chevy pick up truck, five, nine, zero."

"I'll run it and track it down. I'll call you when I have something. He'll be out of town, by now, but unless he has a plan he won't go too far just yet. He'll hide out somewhere and wait. Start checking the nearby towns and look for motels that are run down in the area. Ones that are off the main roads and secluded. When someone grabs a kid, the first thing the police believe is that they try to get away as far as possible. If he's smart, he'll hide out."

"What makes you think he's smart?"

There was nothing smart about showing your face to a witness to grab a kid that was twelve. For all Phillip knew,

River could have fought him or that Sol was in the room as well.

That didn't seem smart to me.

"He's gotta be watching them for him to know when to grab Sol. He probably didn't know what room they were staying in. He wouldn't have been able to get close enough to the motel without being spotted by Sol. But he found them in a small ass town and knew when Sol wouldn't be there. He's going to hide out like a cockroach and wait until the initial shock wears off."

"Okay, we'll start looking. Thanks."

"Always."

I ended the call and I could see the confusion all across Sol's face. He expected me to call the police, not Damien. I couldn't blame him. I remember what I was like when I first got out with my sisters. I didn't trust anyone and I always expected that people would instantly turn on me.

"Thanks, Bobby," I said, before I turned my attention to Sol. "Come on, we have to go."

I knew he was going to have questions and I had no problem answering any of them, but we needed to head out and start looking first. We had to try and track down Phillip, and with some luck, we might be able to find him before Damien was able to track him down by his vehicle. I heard Sol following behind me, and once we got into my car, I spoke before he had a chance to ask any questions.

"Damien says we should look around town at the motels. He thinks Phillip will stay low until he feels it's safe enough to leave. He's going to run the plate and try and track him."

"Damien's a cop?" Sol asked, trying to catch up.

"He's a private investigator. He works with me on the task force."

"Task force?"

This was going to be the problem. I had to tell him the truth. I couldn't lie to him about this. I couldn't lie to him at all. If I did lie, it would break what little trust I had been able to build up with Sol and I didn't want that. I didn't want to lose him. The problem was, though, the truth could make him feel like he couldn't trust me. It could make him feel like he needed to run with River when we got him back and I didn't want that. Because no matter what he did, and I suspected he'd kidnapped River, it wasn't going to change anything for me.

No, that was a lie.

It would change things for me.

It would make me respect him even more. It took a lot of courage to grab your younger sibling and risk everything to keep them safe. I almost couldn't do it, but I knew I had to free as many of my siblings as I could, especially my sisters.

"I work on a task force with some federal agents and local police."

"Wait, you're a cop, too?" Sol asked, confused, but I could also hear the panic starting to set in.

"No. God, no. I'm just a social worker. The task force only goes after criminals that hurt children. They travel all over the country helping as many children as they can. Myself, along with a couple other social workers, help them with placements for the children. We make sure that the children either get to be with their family, or they are placed in a safe and loving foster home. It can be a lot, but we are helping to keep children safe, so it's all worth it. You don't have to worry, Sol, Damien just wants to help people. He'll find Phillip."

I knew for a fact that even if Damien knew the truth, whatever it was, he wouldn't go to the police. Damien and Sebastian, they had a different moral outlook on life. They had no problem overlooking a crime if it was for the better of the world. I knew they had a dark past, whatever it was, and I knew they weren't above burying a body, if that is what needed to be done. I knew I could trust Damien with my own secret and I knew, without a doubt, that Damien would keep Sol's, whatever it was.

"And he said we should look at motels. Wouldn't Phillip have kept driving?"

"Damien believes that he'll find a place close by and stay hidden. That if River's kidnapping was reported, then the police would focus on the direction he could have driven. They won't expect him to hide out nearby. We'll start at one end and work our way through. There's a good number of motels on the outskirts for the tourists."

Sol just gave a small nod and I could feel the anxiety and fear radiating off of him. He was terrified of Phillip having River and I couldn't help but worry and wonder why.

What happened between Sol and Phillip that made Sol this afraid?

And who was Phillip?

Was he an ex-boyfriend, an old friend,

a member of his family?

I had all of these questions, but I knew now was not the time to ask them. Sol wouldn't be ready for any conversations about Phillip until he found River. I just hoped we would find him soon, because I didn't know how long Sol would be able to keep it together.

# CHAPTER SIXTEEN

Isaiah

IT WAS NINETY minutes later when my phone rang.

We had been looking at all of the motels in the area, but so far we hadn't seen Phillip's truck. We had gone in to speak with the front desk workers, but none of them had seen Phillip. With each passing second, I could see that Sol was getting worse. The circumstances were settling in and I knew it was a dark situation.

I knew from working with the task force what happens when a child gets kidnapped. I knew the first twenty-four hours were vital, and I knew I should have called the police. I wanted to give Damien the chance to find Phillip first, though. If he came back with nothing, then I would make the call to Mason. He would be able to help us locate River and, hopefully, he would be willing to look the other way for whatever Sol had done.

"Damien, did you find something?" I asked, once I answered the phone.

"I got his car. It's at a roadside motel about thirty minutes north of town. It's called Sunrise Motel. I'll meet you there."

"We're on our way," I said, and I ended

the call. "Damien found Phillip's car. We're about ten minutes away."

"What are we going to do when we get there?"

Now, that was the question, because I had no clue. Absolutely no clue what we were going to do.

We could knock on the door, assuming we knew which one to knock on, but what if he didn't answer?

What if he had a gun?

What if he wasn't there, or worse, what if River wasn't there?

I had no idea what we were going to do. What I did know was that Damien had said Phillip's truck was at the motel, so that was where we needed to be.

"I don't know, but we can figure it out once we get there. Damien is on his way, so we could always wait for him to arrive and then let him handle it."

That would be the best thing to do. We should wait and allow Damien to take the lead on this. He would know how to handle it and what to do for any number of scenarios. I knew it would be hard for Sol to sit and wait while his brother was most likely in a motel room, but it would be the smarter thing to do in this situation.

"Okay." Sol simply said, but I could hear how unhappy he was with it.

We drove the rest of the way to the motel in silence. Neither of us had anything to say to the other, and there was truly nothing I could say that would make Sol feel any better at this moment, anyway.

Once we arrived, we could see Phillip's beat up pick up truck, so I parked farther away. I didn't want anyone to see us watching the motel room the truck was parked in front of, but at the same time I didn't want to miss anyone coming and going.

I turned my car off and we both sat there with our eyes locked on the motel room door. The blinds were closed on the single window the room had, so we couldn't see if anyone was inside or not. It was only a couple of minutes later when the door to the room opened and a man, Phillip I assumed, walked out with a duffle bag in his right hand and his left hand on the back of River's neck.

Before I could even open my mouth, Sol flung open the door and was climbing out of my car. I couldn't blame him. It looked like Phillip was about to run with River. I quickly got out after him and we approached Phillip.

The man looked over at us as he heard us approach and he instantly dropped his duffle bag. He pulled out a gun from behind his back and pointed it to River's head.

I reached out and placed my hand on Sol's arm to stop him from moving forward. I hadn't been around guns much in my life or career, but I had to complete a course with being on the task force on how to talk down a suspect with a gun. It was mostly geared toward children that wanted to kill their abuser, but I was hoping the basis of the course still applied here.

"Phillip, we don't want any trouble," I started in a calm voice.

"Good, then get the hell out of here and let me take my son home where he belongs," Phillip countered.

"He's not your son," Sol practically growled out.

"Shut up. I don't want to hear your voice. You stole him from me. You broke up our happy family. Everything was perfect until you went and kidnapped my son from me."

I suspected that Sol had kidnapped River and hearing it from Phillip only confirmed it. Still, it didn't change anything. I knew without a doubt that Phillip was dangerous and not safe for River to be around. I hated that we were standing out here without any backup or a way to stop Phillip from using that gun. I wasn't sure that he wouldn't try and shoot one of us.

"Take me instead," Sol said next, and my entire body froze.

# CHAPTER SEVENTEEN

Sol

THE PAST TWO hours had been the most stressful of my life. I hated not knowing where River was and I hated knowing that he was with Phillip. There was no telling what Phillip would do to him. I knew what he was capable of, but I didn't know how he would start it with River.

With me, he came into my room one

night and started to touch me, but I was a bit younger than River and we were on his turf. I also had the threat of River hearing us and getting hurt, so that kept me quiet. River didn't have that threat with being alone with Phillip. The problem was, though, River was twelve and he would be no match against Phillip in a fight.

All I wanted was to be able to see River and make sure he was okay. What I didn't expect was when I finally did find River, there would be a gun held against his head. The second my eyes registered on Phillip, my whole body froze.

I couldn't lose River, not like this.

I had worked so hard to keep him safe, to make sure that men like Phillip never got a hold of him.

I couldn't fail him now.

"Take me instead." The words were out

of my mouth before I could even think.

I would have willingly taken River's place. It wouldn't matter what happened to me as long as River was safe. I couldn't even process the very likelihood that Isaiah now knew that I kidnapped River. None of that mattered. The only thing I cared about was getting River as far away from Phillip as possible.

"I don't want you. I want River. I want my true son. You threw it all away. I did nothing but care for you and for River, but you ruined it. I am not going to allow you to ruin it again," Phillip said with an erratic tone to his voice.

I had never heard Phillip talk this way before. He was always calm and collected. When he did get mad when I fought against him, his voice held a deadly edge to it, but he never sounded crazy.

I had no idea what happened over the past four years, but they had to have been rough on Phillip. I didn't even know he was following us. I always suspected that someone was looking for us, but I thought it would be the police. I never would have figured Phillip to show up. I didn't know what he would do. I figured he would play the role and, eventually, get a new foster child.

I'd refused to allow myself to think about what the next kid would go through, because it was too hard to think about. I always felt guilty and it made me question everything. I had to focus on keeping River safe and hope that someone else down the line would stop Phillip.

"I'm sorry. I didn't mean to upset you like that. I was just a dumb kid and I didn't think it all through. I didn't realize how much you loved us, how much you loved me," I said.

I just needed him to focus on me and take me. I wasn't much of a fighter, but I stood a better chance against Phillip than River did. The problem was, though, I was too old for him and we both knew it. I was also trying to not talk about it with Isaiah there. I didn't want him to know that about me. I didn't want him to learn the whole story. Not like this, at least. If we got out of this, I would have to tell him our story, but that would be on my terms and not Phillip's.

"You knew. You knew how much I loved you, how special you were to me. You took it all for granted. You were ungrateful and you still are!" Phillip yelled.

This situation was quickly getting out

of control and I had no idea how to stop it, how to end it. I wasn't going to let him take River, there was no way in hell that was going to happen.

I knew Damien was on his way, but I didn't know if adding another person into the mix would be the best thing to do, either. Before I could even try and come up with something to say, I heard a voice I didn't expect.

"Put the gun down, Phillip."

I turned to see Max walking between me and Isaiah. I had no idea how he even got here, because he didn't drive. At least, not to my knowledge. What was even more shocking, was he not only knew Phillip by name, but he had a gun in his hand and it was pointed right at Phillip.

"Max?" River asked, softly.

"It's over Phillip. Put your gun down

and let the kid go," Max demanded.

"You would dare point a gun at your father," Phillip growled.

"He's your father?" I asked Max.

I was beyond confused at this point. I thought Max was just another homeless man, but now it looked like he was Phillip's son.

Did that mean Max had been following us, relaying our location back to his father?

Had I trusted my brother to a man that was evil?

None of this was making any sense and I had no idea what to do with this new information.

"Yeah. I've been keeping an eye on him for eight years. When you and River left, he went underground and I knew he would be going after you both. I've been tracking your movements to make sure he never found you."

"How the hell have you been tracking us?" I asked, horrified that someone had been able to follow us this whole time.

I should have seen him.

I should have noticed that someone was watching us. I thought I had been able to keep River safe, and now I discovered I had been failing him this whole time.

"I had been watching the house, waiting for a chance to speak with you. But you left and I was able to track you to that first town. I slipped a GPS tracker in your duffle bag and I've been watching you both ever since. I knew he wasn't going to let you go. I could see it all over his face. I was going to take care of him, but he went under."

I couldn't believe this.

So was Max following us to keep us safe or was he following us because he knew eventually Phillip would find us?

Did it really matter which one it was, though, because the end result was the same.

"You shouldn't be here, Max. You are supposed to be my son. You should be helping me, not pointing that toy gun at me," Phillip said.

Max moved the gun and pointed it at the ground just in front of River and Phillip. He fired one shot and the sound of a gun going off echoed all around us.

"Tell me again how it's a toy. You're gonna put your gun down or the next shot will be in your head. I am not playing," Max said with a deadly edge to his voice.

I had no idea what Max used to do before he decided to stalk River and me for years, but he clearly knew how to handle a gun. I had always suspected he was ex-military, maybe I had guessed right. It would explain how he had access to a GPS tracker.

I was praying that Phillip would put his gun down. I needed to wrap my arms around River and make sure he was okay for myself.

I hated that I felt so useless.

I couldn't do anything to get River away from Phillip.

I hated this.

I just wanted this to end once and for all.

I wanted River safe.

I wanted to be able to live our lives without having to constantly worry about someone finding us.

I could see the uncertainty in Phillip's eyes, but he wasn't foolish enough to doubt Max's promise. Bit by bit, he slowly lowered his gun and the second he tossed it aside, River was at full speed for me. I instantly wrapped my arms around him, pulling him tight to my chest. I made sure to keep him facing behind me so he couldn't see whatever was about to happen.

I had no idea what we were going to do about Phillip, but even if Phillip drove away. River didn't need to see it. He didn't need to see that man for a single second more than he had to.

Being able to finally get my arms around River felt better than anything I could have hoped for. I could feel the slight tremble to his body and I knew it was going to take some time tonight to get him calmed down and no longer feeling scared.

"Are you okay? Did he hurt you?" Isaiah quickly joined us and placed his hands on River and started to check him over as he spoke.

"No, he said we were going for a drive. I'm sorry, Sol," River said with a shaky voice.

"It's okay, you didn't do anything wrong." I was not about to let River blame himself for this. He was a kid, he did nothing wrong.

A sudden shot rang out and it caused all three of us to flinch. I kept my hands on River and looked up to see Phillip falling to the ground with a gunshot right to his heart. I looked over at Max and saw that he was slowly lowering his gun.

"Why?" I couldn't help but ask.

Phillip was his father.

He was unarmed.

He didn't need to shoot him.

Max tucked the gun away into the back of his jeans as he spoke.

"I was his first. I should have done it a long time ago. If I had, a lot of other children wouldn't have been hurt. You should get out of here, take River and head home. I'll handle this mess."

I had no idea how he was planning on handling anything. Damien was on his way and soon the cops would be, too. Even if the motel was empty, the front desk clerk would have heard the two shots. Plus Damien would be here any minute and he would call the police.

This wasn't looking the other way for a robbery, this was murder. Phillip had been unarmed and he wasn't putting any of us in danger any more. Max had killed his own father in cold blood.

Don't get me wrong, I was glad Max killed him. I felt a lot better knowing that Phillip wouldn't be able to find River ever again. River would never know what it felt like to go through the traumatic experiences that I did.

"Come on, Max is right, we need to get River out of here. We can go to my place, it'll be safe there," Isaiah said.

I wasn't sure if I wanted to be at Isaiah's place, if that was the smartest thing to do, but I didn't want to stay here. We couldn't stay here once the cops arrived. I still didn't know what I was going to say or do when they did eventually show up asking questions. You couldn't witness a murder without the police wanting to talk to you. They would know about River's kidnapping and then it was only going to get worse. I didn't know if we'd stay at Isaiah's or not, but at least it was better than standing here waiting to get handcuffs put on me.

"Come on, Bear, let's get out of here," I said.

River was my priority right now.

He was all that mattered.

Isaiah guided us back over to his car and we climbed in. I sat in the back with River as his body was still trembling and I really didn't feel ready to let him go yet.

As Isaiah pulled out of the parking lot, I saw a truck pulling up with a man who I suspected to be Damien. Hopefully, shit wouldn't hit the fan before I had a chance to explain to Isaiah what I had done and, more importantly, why I had done it.

# EVIE RILEY

# CHAPTER EIGHTEEN

Isaiah

I KNEW BRINGING them to my house might not be the smartest decision I'd ever made, but I couldn't stand the thought of them being in the motel room alone.

We did make a quick stop at the motel so they could grab some sleep clothes and River could grab his school stuff. River's trembling seemed to have calmed down a bit by the time we arrived at the motel.

I was hoping that maybe his autism would work in our favor this time with his mind processing what just happened differently. One thing I did know for certain, the last few hours were going to haunt Sol for the rest of his life.

We pulled up to my house and I couldn't help but feel a bit self-conscious over it. The house wasn't bad or anything. It was a very nice house in good condition. It was what the inside would look like. I knew for a fact that my dining room table would be covered in files and even a couple of maps. I knew my kitchen would be clean, but the rest would look lived in.

I did have two extra bedrooms so they would both be able to have a place to sleep tonight that wouldn't involve a couch. I hadn't had anyone over, though, and I wasn't too sure how to handle it myself.

I didn't have visitors, really.

Every now and then, Travis would come over, but for the most part I was alone in my home. It would be different to have someone over, but it also meant I could cook for someone other than myself, which was nice.

The three of us made our way inside and once there, I guided them upstairs as I spoke. "I have two spare bedrooms that you both can use. You are safe here."

I wasn't sure how much comfort that would bring to them, but I wanted to at least try. I showed them to the rooms that were beside each other before I left them alone.

I trotted down the stairs and started to clean up the files that were spread out all over my table. I made sure they were all placed back in the correct folders and then organized them so I could continue with them tomorrow.

With that done, I then turned to my kitchen and started to cook something for dinner. It would not only give River and Sol some time together to talk about what happened with Phillip, it would also give me some time to get my nerves to calm down. Cooking always made me feel better and that was exactly what I needed at this very moment.

While I cooked, though, I couldn't stop thinking about what could have happened between Phillip and Sol. I didn't want to jump to any conclusions, because that wasn't fair to Sol or River. Max had said he killed his father because he was his first and he should have stopped him.

First what, though?

With my line of work, I assumed that could mean only one of two things.

His first abuse victim or his first sex victim.

I was terrified of both options, but the second would be worse. I was hoping, praying, that there wasn't any sexual aspect to it. That Sol or River didn't have to go through anything so horrific. I couldn't imagine if Sol went through anything traumatic like abuse in any form. He seemed like a very sweet young man. He was doing everything he could to take care of his brother, to support him, to give him a home. He didn't deserve to have that type of pain in his life, past or present. I wouldn't be able to talk to Sol until later when we could be alone, but I could make sure they both had a good meal to try and make up for the horrible day they had.

# CHAPTER NINETEEN

Isaiah

IT WAS NEARING nine o'clock by the time Sol came down to join me in the living room.

We had all sat down and enjoyed a simple spaghetti and garlic bread dinner together. It was different, to enjoy a meal with people, but in a good way. Normally, I just worked and ate at the same time.

Surprisingly, River held up the conversation during the meal. He was able to talk about different things he learned from school to fill the silence and prevent it from being awkward.

After everything had been cleaned up, they had gone upstairs to be by themselves for a little while. It gave me some time to work, but finally Sol was now coming down the stairs and I hoped I would finally be able to get some answers to the endless questions going through my mind since this afternoon.

"River fall asleep?" I asked as Sol plopped down on the couch next to me.

"He's reading, so I'll have to go in there in an hour and make him put the book away," Sol said, flashing a small, warm smirk.

"Kids who are as smart as River often

get lost in what they are doing and don't realize how much time has passed. It's good that you make sure he has an alarm set on weekends when you are at work. It will teach his mind to naturally come up for air every three hours even when an alarm isn't set."

He just gave me an awkward nod and I knew he was waiting for when I would ask him about what happened today. I wasn't sure how to bring it up without making it seem like I was interrogating him. Thankfully, he took that away from me.

"I know you have questions about today. It's okay, you can ask them."

Even though he said it was okay, we both knew he didn't really want to talk about it. The issue was, though, we *had* to talk about it. I couldn't leave things as they were, not this time around. It wasn't even about me being their caseworker. It was about me wanting to be his friend and be there for him, to know more about him, and this was my first true chance to learn more about Sol on a personal level.

I couldn't pass it up.

"How do you know Phillip?" I started, and made sure to keep an even balance to my voice, kind of between being gentle and friendly. I didn't want Sol thinking I didn't care, but I didn't want him thinking I was treating him with kid gloves, either.

"He was our foster father. Our only foster father. Our father was never around. He was always in and out of jail and the few times we did see him, he was always drunk and violent. I was seven when River was born and I still can remember how shocked our mother was. She didn't even know she was pregnant.

The doctors were surprised he made it. Even though our mother was around, she wasn't around, you know?"

"I do know. My mother was a lot like that. She was checked out most of the time. She was only fourteen when I was born. My mother was a member of the Fundamentalist Church of Jesus Christ of Latter-Day Saints, or FLDS. They are a religious cult and women there are raised to be nothing more than a breeder. She had ten kids. I was the oldest, so I understand having a parent that is too broken to pay any attention to things like keeping kids alive."

I did know exactly what he felt like. I also knew why he was so close to River. He had taken care of him just like a parent. It was like that with me and my siblings, too. At least, until I was old enough to leave.

"I've heard of the FLDS. I've come across a few ex-members in different cities. They are normally homeless and drug addicts. It's a hard way of life, especially if you are female. The second River was born, he was mine to take care of. I raised him from birth. I would do odd jobs to make enough money to take care of him. I would skip school, sometimes for a week straight and I would forge a note from my mother saying I was sick. When I was eleven, social services finally caught up to us. Figured a kid couldn't be as sick as I always was without it being a problem. They took us both right away."

"And you ended up with Phillip, but how? You both are protected by Native Law, surely there was another home you could have been placed in."

# TORMENTED

I knew not every State had a Native Law they had to follow. However, it was generally customary to place children within their own ethnicity, especially Native Americans. They had different cultures and traditions that were strongly passed down from generation to generation. They should never have been placed with a single, middle aged, white man. Not if the social worker did their job correctly, or cared to do it correctly. Chances were, Sol and River were just another case file to their worker.

"Not in Oklahoma. We were from Holdenville. There were other Natives, but it didn't matter. Most police and social workers grouped all Natives as undesirable. They didn't have any Natives as foster parents and with having no blood relatives, no one could lay claim to us."

"So you went to Phillip," I said with understanding to my voice.

"Everything was great, at first. Even before River was born, I always had to take care of my mother or myself. I always had to worry about having food or water. At Phillip's, though, I didn't have to worry anymore. That first night, he cooked dinner and I remember the whole time I was a nervous wreck because I didn't know what to do. No one had ever cooked for me before. And I think he knew that, because he was really patient with the both of us. He got us in school, he cooked us breakfast and made us lunch every day. It was so perfect. For the first time in my life, I was just a kid. I could go to school and not feel guilty about not having money for food for River."

"That is how it's supposed to be. Whether it's a foster parent or your biological parent, they are supposed to be the one that takes care of you, not the other way around. It didn't last, though, did it?" I asked, but I already knew the answer.

It was a typical abuser play. Treat your potential victim nicely, make them feel special, and then slowly start to abuse them. Make them question their own actions and attitudes. Lower their self-esteem so they will try and do everything the abuser wants them to. It worked very well with children, especially children that came from nothing.

"It did for River, but it didn't for me. One night, he came into my room and started to touch me. At first, I was confused and tried to fight him off, but I didn't stand a chance. It was just touching, at first, but it turned pretty quickly into something more. At first, I wanted to tell someone. I wanted to tell my social worker, but Phillip always treated River perfectly. River was so happy. He was going to school, he always had food, he got to go on field trips and hang out with his friends. For the first time, he was truly happy and I couldn't take that from him."

I could hear the raw pain in Sol's voice. He had endured sexual abuse all so his younger brother would have a proper and loving home. His love for River went deeper than his own need to be safe.

I reached over and took his hand in mine. I could feel him trembling slightly and I knew this was taking a great deal out of him.

"I'm so sorry you had to go through that, Sol. Phillip knew that if he treated River right, then you would be compliant with him. He would have done it before to others. His file would probably show a pattern of him taking in brothers. It would have made it easier for him to control the older brother. Your social worker should have seen the signs, seen the pattern. We can place a child with a single parent, but when an adult male only takes young boys, that's a red flag. They should have stopped him long before you and River got to him."

"We almost never saw our social worker. She stopped showing up after three months. Can't blame her, though, everything was picture perfect fine."

"Until it wasn't. How did you get River out?"

I had a feeling I already knew the answer, but I wanted to give Sol the chance to tell me himself. I felt his body tense at the question and I knew his mind was automatically thinking I would turn him in if he told me. That wasn't going to happen, but he didn't know that. So before he had a chance to speak, I beat him to it.

"When I turned eighteen, I knew I was going to leave the FLDS. The problem was, you couldn't just leave, even once you were an adult. They made sure to keep their members so their numbers would grow. I wasn't going to be staying there. I knew I had to get out, but I didn't want to leave my siblings behind. I gave them all a choice in staying or coming with me. My brothers didn't want to leave. They hadn't discovered how much the life sucked yet. My sisters, though, they wanted out and I wanted them out. The oldest was twelve and my father was already looking to set her up with a husband. The night I left, I took all five of them. We snuck out their bedroom window and ran to the car that was waiting for us. I had managed to connect with an ex-member that helps to get other members out. My sisters were underage, though, and I wasn't their parent, I had no right to take them."

"You kidnapped them," Sol simply stated with complete understanding to his voice.

"I did. And I took them over State lines to Nevada. Nevada had a safe haven law where children who were abused would be protected by the law. They wouldn't have to be taken back to their parents as long as there was proof. With us being within the FLDS, we automatically qualified for protection. My aunt had gotten out a long time ago and she took us all in, no questions asked. Sol, I understand if you did something illegal to save River. It's okay, you can tell me and we can figure it out if we have to. But with Phillip dead, chances are no one is going to be asking questions. You're in the clear. It's okay, you can tell me."

I wanted him to feel safe enough to share with me. I didn't want him to feel like he had to hide something that important. He could tell me anything and I was not about to hold it against him. He did what I did and I would be more than happy to help keep his secret for him.

Sol sucked in a shaky breath before he spoke.

"I started to notice that Phillip was losing interest in me when I was fifteen. I knew what that meant. River was eight, and I noticed Phillip looking at him differently. I knew what he wanted and I had to stop it. I thought about telling someone, but I didn't think anyone would believe me. So one night, I packed our bags and I told River we had to leave. We snuck out his window, hid on a freight train, and we've been running ever since."

I couldn't believe it.

He'd been homeless and taking care of River for four years.

It was insane.

He should never have been put in that position. He never should have had to live his life that way. It was incredible, though, that he had been able to care for River so well at a young age. He didn't kidnap River when they first left home. He was a child himself. However, legally, he was kidnapping River from the age of eighteen on. The fact that it started when he was a minor, though, might work in his favor. I would have to ask Damien and see if there was something that could be done to protect Sol. We could get him custody paperwork from this point forward. I would be looking into it for him.

"You're incredible. At fifteen you were brave enough to take River, a young child, and go on the run to protect him. You've been taking care of River most of his life and he is an amazing young man. You've done remarkably with him, Sol."

"I just wanted him safe. And now he had a gun to his head," Sol said, and I could tell he felt like he had failed River. That was the last thing he had done, though.

"You couldn't have predicted what happened. River is safe and he will overcome what happened. You protected him his whole life and he is an amazing kid. Today is not a loss. It's a win. Phillip can no longer hurt you or River. The both of you are safe now. It'll be okay, Sol." And it would be okay, because I was going to make sure of it.

# CHAPTER TWENTY

Sol

SAFE.

I had never truly been safe before. I wasn't even sure what that felt like. I knew how stupid and pathetic that sounded. Every child was supposed to be able to feel safe in their life and yet, at nineteen, that concept was foreign to me.

I had tried my best to make it possible

for River and living with Phillip had been safe for him.

At least, until I became too old for him.

We didn't have a choice but to leave Phillip's house. I wasn't going to allow River to go through anything that I'd had to. It didn't matter how hard it would be on me, I was going to make sure River was safe more than anything.

I wasn't expecting for Isaiah to be so calm with me about all of this. I knew he must have heard similar stories from his job, but I didn't think he would be so understanding.

He completely understood why I had taken River, why I continued to take him from State to State even after I turned eighteen. He wasn't judging me, he wasn't lecturing me or calling the police. He completely understood, because he did the same thing with his own sisters.

His story was surprising. I had heard about FLDS. I had known that they were a religious cult and favored men over women. I couldn't imagine what it must have been like for Isaiah to have five younger sisters. To know that their fate within the cult was to be abused and forced to have children with men old enough to be their father. He had to get them out and he was brave enough to do it. I had a great deal of respect for him for that.

"What's going to happen to River, now?"

It was the one question I was dreading, because I was terrified of the answer. It was only a matter of time before the police would be asking me questions and arresting me for kidnapping River. There was no way we hadn't been reported missing. Phillip wouldn't have been able to keep it hidden from people. Our teachers would have noticed when we didn't show up for a few days. Social services would be called and they would discover that we weren't with Phillip. I knew I was on borrowed time with River, I just thought maybe we would be able to hold out a bit longer if we stayed smart. Now, my time was almost up and I needed to make sure River would be okay.

"What do you mean?"

"What will happen when the police come to speak with me? Phillip would have reported us missing. They'll know I took him. What will happen to River? Where will he go?"

"No, Honey, he's not going to go anywhere. I promise you. You didn't do anything wrong. You took River with you to keep him safe and you have been able to take care of him for four years while being homeless. No one is going to arrest you for protecting him."

"But I took him," I started to argue, but Isaiah gently cut me off.

"Because his life was in danger. You took him as a fifteen year old, a minor. Even after eighteen, you still felt like he was in danger and you were right. Phillip had been following you. I know a family lawyer. He can draw up some paperwork for you to get you full custody of River. That will cover you from this point forward. And I will speak with my colleagues about getting you immunity for the time since you turned eighteen. We can protect you. I promise no one is going to take River from you."

The determination and strength to his voice had this calming effect on me. I wasn't sure if he would be able to make it possible, but my heart told me to believe him. It told me that he would be able to uphold his word and he wouldn't let me down. Isaiah was a good man, a sweet man, and I would be lying to myself if I said I didn't have feelings for him.

He wasn't what society would dictate as attractive, but to me he was. So many men had used me that the thought of any of them touching me made my stomach turn. Yet with Isaiah, I had often thought about what his touch would feel like. If I would have the same reaction to it as I did the others.

I would never make the first move, though, that would be too risky. I didn't know if he felt the same. He had called me

*Honey* twice now, but that didn't necessarily mean anything. I've had waitresses call me Honey or Sweetie when they took my order.

I wanted him to like me, that was the most shocking part. I wanted him to be calling me *Honey* because I wanted to feel special. I liked Isaiah, as terrifying as it was. I liked him and I desperately hoped that he liked me, too. That it was more than just a professional relationship we shared.

I didn't even know if he was seeing someone. He had never spoken about a boyfriend, or a girlfriend, for that matter, but that wouldn't be uncommon. We had kept things pretty professional between us. We weren't friends meeting up for a drink. He was in my life because he was River's social worker. It was different and there didn't tend to be a personal relationship mixed in.

"I want to believe you. It's hard, though, because life hasn't taught me that good things can happen," I admitted.

"I know, but they do happen. You don't have to do this alone anymore, Sol. I'm here for you and we'll make sure River is safe and secure with you. It'll be okay. Don't worry or stress over it."

That sounded great, but it was hard for me to accept it. I knew, though, only time would tell if he was right or not. I prayed he was, because it would really be nice to not have to worry about being arrested every second of the day.

Isaiah moved his free hand and pushed a strand of my hair and tucked it behind my ear. I had lost my ponytail hours ago and allowed my hair to be free.

I looked at Isaiah and I could see the care in his eyes, the affection within them.

The room suddenly became very silent, but it wasn't awkward. It was as if the whole room disappeared and it was just Isaiah and me. As if we were the only ones in the whole world that existed.

"You are so beautiful," Isaiah said softly, and I had a feeling he wasn't expecting for the words to come out, but I was glad they did.

I wasn't sure who started to move first, but before my mind could even register it, his lips were pressing against mine. Normally, I would recoil and pull away. I usually hated it when someone kissed me. Yet with Isaiah, I was pushing against his lips.

A spark took over my whole body, a feeling that I had never experienced before. I wanted more of it. I had no idea something like kissing could feel this good and I couldn't help but wonder what else Isaiah could make feel good.

I gave a soft moan when I felt his tongue touching my lips, seeking permission to enter, which I easily gave. The second his tongue brushed against mine, I was transported to heaven. I had never felt anything like this before and I never wanted it to end. All too soon, though, Isaiah was pulling back and we were both breathing heavily.

"Sorry, I shouldn't have done that. That was very unprofessional," Isaiah said after a moment.

"Don't be. I've wanted that to happen for a few weeks, now."

"I've wanted to kiss you for a few weeks, now, too. I didn't know you felt the same way and I didn't want to put you in an awkward or uncomfortable position with me being your caseworker."

"I don't care about that. You're a good man, Isaiah. I like you. River likes you, too. He thinks you're fun and smart. You understand a lot more of what he talks about than I do. I didn't really make it far in high school."

"You don't give yourself enough credit, Sol. You're a very smart man, high school diploma or not. You have done amazing with River and I know he appreciates everything you have done for him."

"What happens, now?"

I wasn't sure where we would be going from here. He liked me and I liked him, but did that mean we were dating now?

I was never very good at this part. I hadn't dated anyone. Not while I lived with Phillip and then afterward I was homeless and trying to survive. The only time I had any physical contact with people was when they paid for it. I had never had a boyfriend or been on a date. This whole situation was new to me.

"We take things slow. We don't have to put a label on this, Honey"

That made me feel better. Isaiah wanted to take things slow and I was all for it. I was hoping we could get to know each other and build something real, but I had no idea if that would be able to happen. It would really depend on if I was going to be able to not be arrested. For tonight, though, it was good enough.

# CHAPTER TWENTY-ONE

Sol

"BUT IT'S A school day," River argued and I knew he was not happy with not going to school.

"I know, but after yesterday, I think it would be better for you to be home," I tried to explain.

"But it's a school day," River stated again and I knew this was going to be hard for him.

He liked routines, and now that we knew he was on the spectrum it made sense why he didn't like his routine to be disrupted. Normally, it wasn't a problem, but today I really wanted to have him at the motel. I wanted to make sure it was safe for him to be at school and he needed to process what happened yesterday.

"Morning," Isaiah said as he jogged down the stairs.

"I'm sorry, did we wake you?" We had stayed up last night until about midnight watching a movie before we both turned in. I didn't know when he had to be at work so I had been trying to keep this conversation as quiet as possible.

"Not at all. My alarm goes off at this time. How are you feeling, River?"

"Fine. It's breakfast time, and then

school.”

“I know you love your school, Bear, but I really think you should skip it today. You can do work on the laptop,” I tried to reason once again. Unfortunately, when River got like this it was hard to get him to do anything different. As a rule, that wasn’t a problem, but after yesterday I didn’t know how he would react to the trauma. I wanted him close.

“I’ll make some eggs,” Isaiah simply offered.

I had been hoping for some of his support on this, but apparently, he was leaving this to me.

River headed up the stairs to get dressed before I could say something else to him. Letting out a sigh, I made my way to the kitchen to join Isaiah.

“He shouldn’t be going to school,” I

started.

"And if he was an average child I would completely agree with you. But with his autism, he takes comfort in routine. It might be best for him to go to school and live his life just like he usually does."

"And if it all hits him? What if he gets to school and has a problem? He needs time to process what happened to him."

Isaiah placed his hand on my hip as he spoke. "I understand why you're worried, but keeping River away from his routine might make him worse. He takes comfort in his routine so any disruption to it could make him more anxious and aggravated. If you want, I could call the school and speak with the Headmistress. I can inform her about River being grabbed by Phillip and that he was safely rescued. She will inform his teachers and the counselor will be able to keep an eye on him. If a problem comes up, they will know how to handle it."

I knew the school had good counselors that handled anything that came their way. River really liked his, but it still made me nervous for people to know what happened to River.

"What would you say about Phillip?"

"Just that he was an unstable foster parent before you got custody of River. I'll keep it vague and simple. I'm assuming you never told River about the true reason why you left."

"No, I never told him. I just said it wasn't safe and he's never asked. One day, I'll tell him, but I don't think he could handle the news just yet."

"No, it would be best to wait on that one. I know it's hard, but the best thing the both of you can do would be to go about your day like you always do. Let River go to school and you go to work. You can both come back here tonight and we can have dinner. That is, if you want."

"I would love to."

More than anything, I would love to come back here tonight and share a meal with him again. Isaiah was not only a very good cook, but he was great company. He made me feel cared for. He made me feel smart. He made me feel safe, and that was the biggest draw for me. He made me feel safe, and after not being safe for my whole life, I wanted nothing more than to keep feeling safe.

"It'll be okay. River will go to school and he'll have a great day. The best thing you can do for him right now is to allow him to go at his own pace. This will hit him, but it has to happen on his terms."

That was what I was scared of. That it would happen when I wasn't there to help him through it. I didn't want River to have to feel like he was all alone when his mind kicked in to what happened to him. I wanted him safe. I wanted to protect him from the entire experience. Only, I couldn't now. All I could do was try and keep him together and not fall apart.

I hated this.

"All right, I'll let him go, but I'm not happy about it."

Isaiah offered me a warm smile before he leaned in and placed a gentle kiss on my cheek before he spoke. "He'll be okay. I'll make the call shortly to let his Headmistress know. They'll keep an eye on him and if something is wrong, they'll call you."

Not worrying wasn't going to happen, but at least River would be happy with getting to go to school. I had no idea how well today was going to go over, but at least I'd be at work and could, hopefully, turn my mind off to everything that was going on. I just hoped that there were no problems today with River. We could both use a good day.

# CHAPTER TWENTY-TWO

Isaiah

IT WAS AROUND noon when my phone started to ring non-stop between Mason and Damien calling me. I knew it was going to be about what happened yesterday. It was a conversation I had been hoping could be delayed a day or two, but it looked like that wasn't going to be possible.

I had finally given in and answered Mason's call. He was technically my boss when I was working for the task force. It was how I ended up out front of Damien's private investigation business for a meeting that was going to be a very long one.

The good thing about this was, I would be able to ask them both about Sol and what help we could give him. He wasn't in the wrong and I didn't want him to have to live with the threat of being arrested for the rest of his life. I was already doing that and I knew how much it sucked at times.

Letting out a slow and deep breath, I strolled inside ready to go to war, if that was what it took. I was going to make sure that Sol was protected. I wasn't going to allow him to be punished for doing the right thing by his brother. Yes, it was simple for some to say that he could have told someone, that he could have gone to the police. But I knew for a fact it wasn't that simple.

Children almost never reported it. They almost never talked about it. They endured and they were either destroyed by it, or they pushed through and tried to put it behind them. Sol was doing that, he was doing his best to raise his brother and be a good man. He deserved to have a fair chance at life and to be happy.

I walked into Damien's office and saw that Mason was there, but so was Max. I didn't see Sebastian anywhere, so I assumed he must have given us privacy for this conversation. I wasn't expecting to see Max here, but it made sense. He did have a great deal to do with what happened yesterday.

"Thank you for joining us, Isaiah," Mason started.

I couldn't tell if he was angry or not. Mason had an amazing poker face and most people almost never knew what he was thinking or feeling. It could be hard to know where anyone stood with him, but as long as he didn't say anything negative, you knew he was okay with you. It took a bit to get used to, but I was good with working for a variety of people and personalities.

"Of course. What would you like to discuss?" I asked as I made my way around to slip into a free seat at the table.

"I think you know exactly what we need to discuss," Mason said with a deadly serious tone. He wasn't in the mood for anyone playing dumb today.

"Max was about to give us his side of things," Damien said, jumping to my rescue, which I greatly appreciated.

"Phillip and my mother didn't stay together long. She didn't like how he acted toward her. He was never violent, but he didn't care to have a wife. She left when I was four and she never came back. I was eight when he started to touch me for the first time. By the time I was nine, he was raping me almost every other day and it went up from there. When I was fifteen, he sent me off to a private school in another State. I was too old for him, but at the time I didn't think much of it. It wasn't until I was an adult did I discover that he had gotten a foster kid within months of me being in school," Max started.

"How many before River and Sol?" I

asked.

"His file had ten others before them. When they got too old, he would ship them off or come up with a reason for the transfer out. They were his first siblings. Generally, it was only one boy at a time. It made it easier for when they started to act out as a teenager. I had been keeping an eye on Phillip, but he tended to move from one State to the next so the foster system wouldn't notice the pattern. I found him just after Sol and River left. I broke into his house when he was at work and saw that he was trying to find them. He was obsessed with Sol and I knew he wasn't going to let them go. He gave me the slip and I started to follow Sol and River around. I stayed hidden in the background, and that was the first time I had reached out to them."

"Why?" Mason asked this time.

"Sol seemed like a good guy. He had been working hard on keeping River alive, taking care of him. He put his own pain behind him so he could focus on River. He looked like he needed a friend, so I made myself known to him. I was planning on telling him about who I was, but then Phillip grabbed River and I wasn't about to let him get away with causing any more pain. I kept tabs on Phillip while I was watching Sol and River. He had hurt other kids while he was chasing after them. He grabbed kids that were homeless, orphans living in group homes, kids that no one cared about. He would use them for as long as he could, before he would kill them. The kids would turn up weeks, sometimes months later. All are cold cases."

"How do you know it was Phillip?" Damien asked.

I was getting a sinking feeling in the pit of my stomach. To know that Phillip not only abused more kids, but he had killed them to cover up his tracks.

It was disgusting.

Children were supposed to know what it was like to be safe.

They weren't supposed to know that monsters were real.

"He was the last person to see the kids alive. He also had a signature. He liked to bite and leave his mark on his victim's private area. He didn't just nibble, he bit down hard enough to scar. It was his way of claiming someone as his own and making sure they were ruined for anyone that came after. In four years, twenty-six kids were found with that scar on them.

The Feds never picked them up because it was all over the Country and the M.E just figured they were being experimental. Most of the kids were between twelve and fifteen, so it's not unlikely that they had sexual partners."

I wanted to be sick.

I couldn't help but wonder if Sol had that same scar.

Was he marked by Phillip or did that come after?

I already knew the answer, because if Max knew about the scar, that meant it was something he had always done and Sol didn't escape that painful reminder.

"Why didn't you ever report it?" Mason demanded.

"I did. No one cared. I reported it to my old boss at the FBI. He told me I was paranoid and needed to get some help. No one was going to do anything, so I made sure I took care of it," Max said with a deadly edge.

I was surprised that he had worked for the FBI. I didn't expect for him to be an ex-federal agent. I thought maybe military, he had that look, but not law enforcement.

If he had been in the FBI, then why did he kill Phillip in cold blood?

And what happened that made him either leave the agency or be fired from it?

I had more questions than answers now, but I doubted I would ever get answers from him.

"You're an ex-fed, why did you kill an unarmed suspect?" Mason asked.

"Because he needed to be put down. Are you really going to tell me you haven't wanted to kill a sick son of a bitch that you've come across? Come on, Mason, how many times have you had to go into hell and see children abused, tortured, and treated like a piece of shit, only for their abuser to go free over some technicality? How many have you seen able to play the system and get off with just a slap on the wrist? I wasn't about to let that happen. Phillip needed to be put down and I would do it again. No regrets or remorse."

I could tell that Max meant every single word. He had no problem killing his own father in cold blood. There was a deep physiological wound within Max and it wouldn't be healed until he sought help for it. I wasn't getting the impression that Max wanted the help, though.

"I know you're not happy with this, Mason, but Phillip was a pedophile. He needed to be put down. We weren't going to have anyone that could testify against him. Max is too old and everyone else is dead. There's no one that could testify against him in court. He was going to get to continue to rape and kill children. There were no witnesses to the murder outside of Isaiah and Sol. I highly doubt Sol is going to talk and report his death," Damien started.

Sol wasn't going to be saying anything, just like I knew River wouldn't be, either. The two of them would be happy to bury this. They didn't know that Sol was a victim and he was still within the statute of limitations. They didn't need to know that, though, because it would only make things worse. I doubted that Sol would testify. I couldn't see him sitting in a courtroom and telling his story, especially when his story ended with kidnapping.

"He won't. Sol has too much to lose. He's not going to risk losing River. If you want to bury this, then you won't get any complaints from me."

I wasn't certain if that is what Mason was looking to get done. I knew Max and Damien were hoping for that outcome, but it wouldn't be granted unless Mason agreed to it. I didn't know Mason well enough to know if he would let this one slide. He typically always followed the law, but he had, on occasion, looked the other way if the ends justified the means. Mason let out a long and hard breath before he spoke.

"Fine, but this is on you, Damien. As long as he's in this town, you're responsible for him." Mason held his hand up to stop Damien from protesting.

"You took that responsibility on when you helped him cover up a murder. You helped him dig the grave. As long as he's in my town, his actions fall on you." Mason turned to give Max his full attention as he continued. "I suggest you remember that the next time you feel trigger happy."

I was surprised that Mason had agreed to bury it. But at the same time, the only thing he could do would be to dig up Phillip and arrest both Max and Damien.

The task force relied on Damien and his men to help with leads and generating informants. He couldn't throw that away for nothing. Murder wasn't nothing, but it became less important when you were dealing with someone like Phillip.

"Fine," Damien said, and it was clear he wasn't happy.

"There is one thing I do need some help with," I started. I needed to talk to Mason about this, but I wasn't sure if now would be the best time. However, he just looked the other way for murder, so now seemed like a great time to bring up kidnapping.

"What?" Mason asked, and I could see he was a bit apprehensive about of what I might have to say.

"I talked to Sol last night and got the full story. Phillip had been molesting him since he was eleven when he became their foster father. He left when he was fifteen, River was eight, when Phillip started to gain an interest in River. They ran away and they have been running for the past four years. Sol has taken River across multiple State lines even after he turned eighteen."

"Oh good, kidnapping, fabulous," Mason said sarcastically.

"At least it's not murder," Damien said with a smirk that quickly disappeared with a sharp look from Mason.

"I know it's not that great, but he took River when he was a minor. And now we know he had every reason to keep running even after he turned eighteen. Phillip had been after them, and if Sol went to the authorities they wouldn't have allowed him to keep River. They would have put River with foster parents, making River vulnerable to Phillip and other predators. Sol didn't do it out of malice, he did it to protect River," I said in Sol's defense.

"I am assuming you are looking for an immunity letter from me," Mason stated.

"Yes. I am going to meet with Jay to get

Sol legal custody of River, but it would help if Sol didn't have to worry about kidnapping charges being laid against him."

Mason let out a sigh before he spoke. "I'll draft it. He was a minor when he left and, as you pointed out, he did have a reason to be on the run. I'll get the paperwork in order today and file it."

"Thank you. I greatly appreciate it and I know Sol will, as well," I said, flashing him a warm smile.

"You're welcome. Now, if no one else would like to confess to a felony, I'm going to leave," Mason said, and stood. When no one said anything he strolled out the door without looking back.

I couldn't blame him, he did just decide to cover up a murder and then correct a kidnapping. It had been a long day for him already, and it was only half over.

I wasn't sure what to make of Max, but he wasn't my problem to figure out. I didn't know how much Damien would appreciate having to keep an eye on Max, but he seemed to be willing. It was his decision and he had clearly made it.

"Thank you for what you did to protect Sol and River. I truly appreciate it," I said to Max. I might not approve of what he had done, but I was glad that Phillip was dead and couldn't hurt Sol or River ever again.

"Don't mention it. Seriously, don't mention it," Max said with a slight edge to his voice. He then stood and headed out the door.

"Are you going to be okay with having to be accountable for him?" I asked

Damien once we were alone.

"It should be fine. He'll probably leave town, anyway. How are Sol and River?"

"River doesn't seem to have processed what happened, yet. He's on the high end of the autism spectrum, so I don't know how he will process it. Sol, he's been through a lot, but I think he's trying to be okay again. Maybe be okay for the first time in his life."

"It's a lot to take for someone. It'll take time, but he should get there. The both of them will, I'm sure. As for River, maybe it's a good thing his mind works differently. Maybe he won't realize what happened, what it truly means. Only time will tell, unfortunately. You gonna be okay? You've taken a liking to both River and Sol."

Leave it to Damien to be able to see

through my emotions. Seeing that gun to River's head, I was certain it took off a decade from my life. The fear of not knowing what was going to happen, I thought my heart was going to stop. I meant what I said to Max, I was grateful for him taking that shot. I couldn't imagine how hard it would have been for Sol to fight against Phillip in court. I didn't want him to have to go through that, and now he wouldn't have to.

"He's a good man and River is a sweet kid. I'll be fine. They are now safe and Sol won't have to worry about being arrested. They can finally live their lives without fear."

"And your romantic feelings for Sol?"

"We kissed for a moment last night. He has feelings for me as well. We're going to take things slow. He's been through a lot.

We don't need to rush anything."

That was what I was afraid of. I didn't want him to feel pressured into anything sexual. It would have to be a conversation we had before anything further could happen between us. I wanted to make sure he knew there was no pressure from me.

I would be telling him that I was a virgin. After everything he told me about his past, it was the least I could do and it was only fair. I also knew he wouldn't hold it against me. He wouldn't poke fun because I was still holding onto it. He would understand how precious it was and I knew he would accept me for it.

It was a conversation we would have shortly, but it wasn't one that needed to be had right away. We had all the time in the world, now.

340

# CHAPTER TWENTY-THREE

Sol

I HAD NO idea I could be this nervous. It was just dinner, that was all we were doing, and yet, I was more nervous, now, than I had ever been.

It had been a week since Phillip had kidnapped River.

A week since Isaiah had kissed me and changed my life completely.

For the past week, things had been happening very fast. I was now cleared of my potential kidnapping charges. Isaiah had gotten Mason, the head of the task force, to give me complete immunity for taking River across State lines since I was eighteen. Having that single piece of paper meant everything to me.

It meant we didn't have to leave and keep running to avoid being detected by the police.

It meant that River would never be taken away from me.

It also meant I could finally breathe and not have to constantly look over my shoulder.

I could finally relax.

I had also met with Jay, a family lawyer in town, and he was helping me to get all of my paperwork in order so I could have legal custody of River. It was a formality, but it made me feel better to have it. It meant it was official, I was River's guardian and he was my responsibility.

Isaiah was helping me from a professional end of things. He was vouching for me in court about my parenting skills and what I had done for River for years.

I still couldn't believe all of this had happened. I never expected for my life to change this much when we came into town. I expected to be here for six months, max, and now, we were building a life here.

Building a home here.

River was in love with his school and he even had a good group of friends that he was often hanging out with on the weekends. I had a real job and I was going to be able to have a job with Jason and make very good money working different job sites.

I even now had a boyfriend.

Something I never thought I would have and yet, I did.

Isaiah was a great man. He was very sweet and gentle, something I greatly appreciated. He was leaving all of the control in the bedroom in my hands. It would be my decision when we took things to another level and I couldn't even express how relieved and happy it made me feel.

All too often in my life, I had been given no choice about what would happen to my body. Phillip took whatever he wanted without any care about what I wanted or how I felt. The Johns I had picked up were paying me and they only cared about what their own pleasure could be. I was just a live action sex toy to them.

It meant everything to me that Isaiah was allowing me to dictate what we did.

I wasn't sure when I would ever be ready to have sex with Isaiah, but I was open to trying different activities with him. I was interested in kissing him again, and seeing what his hands would feel like on my body. If his lips felt that amazing, I knew his hands would as well.

We had to talk about it first, though, because he deserved to know that I had been a prostitute in the past. It wouldn't be fair to him for me to keep something like that from him. It was different than having different sexual partners or a lot of ex-boyfriends. I had sold my body to strangers, and that took things to a whole new level that Isaiah deserved to know.

"You are going to wear a hole in the floor with all of that pacing you are doing," Max commented from his spot on my bed.

He was currently sitting against the headboard in his new clothes. I was both surprised and not surprised to discover that Max had been a federal agent. I always figured military, but being a federal agent also made sense.

Turned out, he had a great deal of money and didn't need to be homeless. He was currently staying in the motel, just three doors down from me, until he decided what he wanted to do. He was wearing his new clothes: black, straight cut jeans and a black t-shirt. His black leather jacket was hanging off the back of the chair and his black biker boots were sitting by the door. I also knew that tucked into the back of his jeans, hidden by the hem of his t-shirt, was his nine millimeter gun. I wasn't sure how I felt about him being armed around River, but I also knew he was safe to have around him.

I had found Max a couple days after he had killed Phillip. I wanted to thank him and make sure he knew that I appreciated everything he had done for me. Isaiah had come home that first day and told me all about the meeting between him, Mason, Damien, and Max. He had told me that Max had been following us around for years and that was when things started to make sense.

There had been a few times when I was in a fight, got jumped, technically, but someone had jumped in to help me. I never saw their face, it was always dark and the world spun from my position on the ground. But I did remember someone had always happened to jump in to help me. I suspected that person was Max.

I owed him my life a few times over.

I could trust him and he didn't deserve for me to hold any of his past actions against him.

He had never hurt us.

He had protected us, and that was all I needed to know.

"Sorry," I said as I sat down on the edge of the bed and let out a deep sigh.

"It's just dinner, Sol."

"I know, and I know it shouldn't be a big deal, but I've never gone on a date before. What if I do the wrong thing or say the wrong thing?"

I was so afraid that I was going to screw this up before it even started. I didn't want Isaiah to see me as broken and I was worried that he would only ever view me as that.

"Look, the first date is always the hardest. You just have to remember that it's no different than going out for dinner with a friend or River. Isaiah is a guy, just like you. You don't have to worry about being romantic. Romance will come later. Be yourself and relax, Kid. And if it helps, Isaiah is probably just as nervous as you are. From what I've observed, he doesn't go out on many dates."

*Kid.*

That was Max's new nickname for me.

I wasn't too sure about it at first, but I knew he didn't mean it in a degrading way. It was his way of showing that he cared. It was weird when I thought about it, because, technically, Max had watched River and me grow up for the last few years. He'd done it from a distance and I couldn't help but wonder what it was like for him. He seemed to know all about us, but I knew nothing about him. He already had a connection to us, but we were just building our own with him.

"That makes no sense, though, because Isaiah is a great guy. How could he not have been on dates or have lots of boyfriends?"

Max gave a small, deep chuckle in his throat before he spoke. "Because society is shallow. Guys look at Isaiah and they see his appearance before they get to know him. You don't do that. It's good that you don't. He seems like a good guy and as long as he treats you right, that's all that matters."

"There's nothing wrong with his appearance, though. Just because he doesn't have a six pack doesn't mean he's unattractive. There's nothing wrong with a bit of chubbiness."

To me, Isaiah was sexy. I loved how he looked and I wouldn't change anything about him. I didn't care about what society wanted to dictate was acceptable or hot. That didn't matter to me. A person could have the best body in the world and be completely ugly on the inside. If someone wasn't a beautiful person internally, then it didn't matter what they looked like on the outside. True beauty lay within, and that was all I cared about.

"There isn't. But the fact that you know that is what makes you a great guy. Don't worry about tonight. Just focus on having fun. You deserve it, Kid."

I looked over at Max and saw a small warm smile touching his face. Now that he wasn't playing homeless, I could see the deadliness in his eyes, in his body. I knew without a doubt that Phillip wasn't the first person he had killed and covered up.

When Isaiah told me that they were covering up the murder, I didn't even hesitate to agree to go along with it. Phillip was dead and that was the only thing I cared about. I wasn't about to put Max in a grind because he did what was needed.

"Thank you for everything you've done for me and River. Isaiah told me you've been looking out for us. It was you that saved me those times when I was attacked, wasn't it?"

"It was, and you got nothing to thank me for. It was my father that you were on the run from. I should have killed him years ago and then you never would have had to go through the shit you did."

"You were a victim, too. You didn't know what would happen and when you were strong enough you went after him. What I don't understand, though, why didn't you stick around all of those times? You were following us anyway, you could have made yourself known. Why stay in the shadows?"

Yes, at first I would have been apprehensive with him, but I was also fifteen and would have loved the help, the protection of having someone else there with us. He would have been twenty-six at the time. He would have known things that could have helped us.

"Phillip wouldn't have shown his face if he knew I was with you. I had to stay hidden, it was the only way to get him. I still have friends with the FBI and this task force was getting one hell of a name for itself. Not just for arresting criminals, but creating a safe haven for those that needed protection. I knew you and River would be safe here, but I needed to get you here. I had Dirty Harry tell you about this town, knowing that you would come here with River. I did my research and got here just before you did. I knew you would want to stay, so I made myself known. It was only a matter of time before Phillip caught wind of you and came down here. I didn't expect it to be that fast, though, or I would have had eyes on River the whole time."

I couldn't believe what I was hearing.

The only reason River and I were even in town was because Dirty Harry had said there was a great opportunity for work here. It was all a ploy by Max to get us here. To get us into a town that would have people in it that would help us.

It was all because of Max that we both had a real shot at life, now.

I owed him everything.

"I am glad that you had us come here and that you finally showed yourself. You're a good man, Max, and we are lucky to have you in our lives," I said, flashing him a warm smile.

"I'm lucky to have you both," he said, and flashed his own warm smile just as the bathroom door opened.

River had been in the shower and he was looking forward to spending some time with Max. Max was going to be watching River while I was out on my date. I didn't know how long it would go on for and I was nervous about leaving River alone in the motel room after what happened. Max had been more than willing to hang out with River.

"You're still here?" River asked as he sat down on his bed.

"I'm heading out, now. You have fun with Max," I said as I stood.

"We're gonna have a blast. Literally, we're going to design a robot that will blow stuff up. Those other robotic teams are going to go home crying at the next tournament," Max said, flashing a deadly smirk.

That should concern me, but Max had more than proved himself to be trustworthy with River. Maybe every kid needed a deadly killer in their corner. It would certainly make them safer.

"Don't blow up the room," I said as I grabbed my coat.

"It's only in theory," River commented as he opened his laptop.

"Hey, Sol," Max said just as I went for the door.

I turned to give him my full attention before he continued.

"Remember to have some fun, Kid."

"I will try my best," I promised before I strolled out. I had no idea how well dinner would go over, but I was hoping that maybe afterward I would get a bit of dessert.

# CHAPTER TWENTY-FOUR

Sol

"CAN I GET you something to drink?" Isaiah asked, once we walked into his home.

Dinner had gone very well. Better than I thought it would. We had gone to a casual restaurant, so it wasn't romantic or too overwhelming for the both of us. I could tell that Isaiah was just as nervous as I was, just like Max had said. It made me feel better to know that I wasn't the only one feeling nervous or unsure about how it all worked. We had gotten through it, though, and it was a lot of fun once the nerves disappeared.

We had decided to come back to Isaiah's place so we could talk more. I was now nervous about the conversation we were going to have. It seemed like Isaiah was thinking the same thing. But I knew we needed to have this conversation in order for us to move any of the sexual aspects of our relationship along.

"No, I'm good. Thanks."

The last thing I wanted was a drink. I wanted to get this over and done with so we could hopefully kiss for a little while. We went and sat down on his couch and I quickly spoke before the awkwardness set in.

"I've never had a boyfriend before."

If Isaiah was surprised, he didn't show it. He kept his face calm and understanding, and I appreciated that. I didn't want any judgments or sympathy from him.

"I had a feeling you hadn't dated, given everything that happened to you. I have only had a couple of boyfriends myself. They didn't last long and they weren't serious. I will be honest with you, Sol, I've never had sex. I am a virgin."

That shocked the hell out of me.

He was actually a virgin.

How was that even possible?

He was sexy, smart, kind. He had a job and he could cook. What was there not to like about him?

"How is that even possible? You're

amazing. You should have a line of guys wanting to be with you."

Isaiah let out a small chuckle. "Far from it. After I got out of the FLDS at eighteen, I focused on my education and getting my Master's degree. I didn't know how to interact with people outside of the FLDS, so I didn't go to parties or experiment with drinking or drugs. After college, I was working and didn't really know how to flirt or pick up a guy. I've had a couple of boyfriends, but they didn't want to take things slow and, eventually, my inexperience annoyed them. For me, I have always believed that losing your virginity isn't something you should take lightly. It should be shared between two people that care for each other. Now, I'm older and it's weird."

"I don't think it's weird. Uncommon,

maybe, but that doesn't make it weird. I think it's nice that you want it to be with someone you care for. It's not something that should be taken lightly or for granted."

I wish I had been able to pick the person I wanted to lose my virginity to. It wouldn't have been with Phillip, that's for sure, and it wouldn't have been so violent and painful. I hated that I had to have that as my first memory of sex and the men that came after weren't much better.

People always talked about how amazing sex was, but that hadn't been my experience, yet. I hadn't reached the amazing part where sex was concerned.

I wanted to, though.

I wanted that so badly.

I wanted to know what it felt like to be with someone that I chose and that cared enough about me to give me my own pleasure. I hadn't even gotten off by someone else, yet. The only time I had ever had an orgasm was by my own hand and never during sex.

I wanted earth-shattering sex.

The kind that left your legs all numb and tingly.

"Have you been with anyone after Phillip?" Isaiah asked me gently.

"I have, yes, but not a boyfriend. When times were hard, and I wasn't able to get a cash job, I would prostitute. Only when there was no other choice and we needed money for food. There's been about thirty guys," I admitted, and I couldn't help but lower my eyes in embarrassment and shame at the admission.

Isaiah placed his hand on my chin and lifted it up as he spoke. "You don't have anything to be ashamed of, Honey. You did what you needed to do in order to survive. You should never have been put in that position. You have nothing to be embarrassed about. It doesn't bother me. What you had to do in order to keep you and River alive, I understand. And it's all in the past, now. You don't have to do that anymore."

"I hated it. I would close my eyes and wait for it to be over. I didn't want to do it, but then I would look at River and remember he hadn't eaten in two days."

"You didn't do anything wrong, Honey. I'm sorry you had to go through that, especially after everything you went through with Phillip. You should never have been put into that position. I need you to know that I would never pressure you into doing anything with me. I don't care how slow we take things in the bedroom."

I felt a weight lift off of my shoulders at hearing those words. He understood fully why I did what I did, and he wasn't disgusted by it. This man was amazing and I couldn't believe how lucky I was to have him in my life.

"I'm glad you want to take things slow. I like you and I don't want you to feel pressured with me. I'm in no rush to have sex." I flashed him a shy smile.

"I'm not, either. I like you, too, and nothing else matters."

It warmed my chest to hear that he wanted me and it didn't matter if we had sex or not. He genuinely cared for me, and that only made him more attractive.

I easily leaned in and placed my lips against his. He quickly responded and moved his hand up to cup my cheek in his large palm as he deepened the kiss.

I let out a soft moan as his tongue slid over mine. I would never get tired of this feeling, of his lips against my own. I wanted more than just his lips tonight. I wanted to feel him against me.

I moved over to straddle his lap without ever breaking the kiss. Once I settled onto his lap, I pulled back just ever so slightly and spoke.

"This okay?"

"More than okay," Isaiah said, his voice breathy, before he pulled me back down for a kiss.

I moved my hands to the back of his neck and eagerly kissed him back. Our tongues danced with each other and Isaiah moved his hands down my back and rested them on my ass.

I rocked my hips ever so slightly, but it was enough to make us both moan at the contact as our hard dicks rubbed against each other. That was all Isaiah needed before he started to take a bit more control.

He squeezed my ass and pulled me closer to him. My whole body felt like it was on fire and there was nothing that could put it out. Every time his body touched mine, the fire grew until it swallowed me whole.

"You feel so good. I had no idea it could feel this good," I moaned as we pulled back just enough to get some air.

"It gets better," he promised.

"Show me," I said softly against his lips.

Isaiah crushed his lips against mine and I started to rock my hips. He pulled me tighter against him with the control he had on my ass. I moaned as I easily pushed my hips down so our cocks rubbed against each other. I could feel how hard he was through his pants and it only turned me on more.

Isaiah moved his hands around to my front and started to undo my pants. That was all I needed to take my own action and start undoing his. Once both of our pants were undone, his hand was slipping underneath my boxers and pulling my hard dick out.

I let out a deep, throaty moan as his skin touched me.

This was better than anything I had ever experienced before in my life. I quickly did the same to Isaiah and I was rewarded by a deep moan bubbling from his throat.

He felt amazing in my hand and he was large. Quite possibly the largest I had felt. It should have scared me, but it only turned me on more. I groaned, panting as Isaiah worked my dick. He was very good at this.

"That's it, Honey, just feel," Isaiah said as he broke the kiss and started to feather his lips along my neck.

All I could do was feel.

My whole body was on fire.

It was as if every pleasure sensor that I possessed was wide awake and screaming for more. Like I had been starving for years and now I was getting an all you can eat buffet.

I could feel my own orgasm rising and I could tell that Isaiah was getting close as well. He was getting harder and he could no longer keep kissing my neck. We were both breathing heavily and it was only a moment later when I gave a deep moan as I came harder than I ever had before.

"Isaiah…"

I wasn't sure what pushed him over the edge, but he followed right behind me. My whole body was tingling as we both continued to moan and pulse in the other's hand. Never had I ever felt this good before. I had no idea a person could feel this good. I could quickly become addicted to this and I was not the least bit worried.

When we finally finished pulsing, or breaths returning to a more normal level, I opened my eyes. I had no idea when I closed them, and I looked up just in time to see Isaiah take his hand away from my semi-hard dick and bring it up to his mouth. He ran his tongue over his digits and licked up the cum that had dripped onto it. I moaned at the sight and I could feel myself getting hard all over again.

"You taste so sweet," he moaned and flashed me a cocky grin, and that broke everything in me.

I captured his lips once again and quickly began to explore his mouth with my tongue. I moaned at the taste of myself all over his tongue as he hungrily kissed me back. When we finally ran out of air, we pulled apart and he spoke.

"I'm nowhere near done with you tonight."

"Good," I said with a flirty smirk as I brought my own hand up and licked at the cum he left on it.

Tonight was all about fun and I was looking to explore everything that Isaiah could do to my body.

# TORMENTED

# CHAPTER TWENTY-FIVE

Isaiah

IT HAD BEEN six weeks since Sol and I had started our relationship. So far, things had been great. We were able to be open with each other and talk about what we had done sexually in the past. I was letting Sol dictate our pace in the bedroom.

Even though I was ready to take things

further, to have sex with him, it was important to me to make sure that Sol was ready for that. He had never really gotten much say in it. He didn't have a boyfriend before or during his years with Phillip. Afterward, any man that he had been with was to keep him and River alive. He didn't get a say in who wanted to pay him to have sex. It was important to me that if and when we had sex, it would be Sol's decision.

Today, I was going to meet up with Travis and speak with him about our group home. We were finally making progress in the sense that we now had approval from the town to build one.

The process was a lot slower than I'd anticipated, but I knew it would be worth it once we got it up and running. We still had a great deal that we needed to make decisions on, not to mention plan. It was a process that we could now at least start.

We were meeting at a coffee shop and not his home. I was still trying to get a peek inside his house and I was constantly denied. He never flat out said no, though. He always had a reasonable excuse. I knew it was perfectly logical that the excuses were real, but I couldn't help this nagging feeling like he was trying to come up with a reason for me to not be in his home.

I arrived at the coffee shop and saw Travis was already here and sitting down at one of the booths. I quickly grabbed my order and made my way over to him. The table already had files all over it and I knew it was going to be a long meeting. That was okay, though, because it would mean that we had gotten a lot accomplished. Travis gave me a warm smile as I slid into the booth across from him.

"Morning. I appreciate you agreeing to meet here. My home is a mess right now with all of the painting."

"Not a problem. What color are you painting?"

"Just a fresh coat of white. It's an old house and all of the walls have that brown tint to them from the white paint getting dirty."

"I know what you mean. I had to repaint mine a year ago. It was a lot of work and hassle."

See, a reasonable excuse, but it was one of many with Travis so it got to be hard to tell when he was being honest or not. I suppose it didn't really matter, but I wanted to make sure he knew that he could tell me anything, good or bad.

"That it is, but it should be worth it once it's done. At least, that is what I keep telling myself. Anyway, I have spoken with Dominic and he is all set to help out wherever we need. He is even helping with capital with his connections."

"That would be great if he can help us with fundraising. Did he say if he wanted to be more involved or just help in the initial phase?"

It would be nice to have Dominic on our side long-term. Obviously, someone that could help with keeping capital within the group home was vital. However, Dominic would be great to have around for other reasons.

We needed to have people working for the group home for free. People that would be able to put together events to help generate funds. People that could work connections and help us with organizing the children that would be at the group home.

We would also need to hire someone to live with the children and help take care of them. Potentially, multiple people to help, depending on how big we could make it.

We would also need to find volunteer therapists that could see the kids and make sure they were doing well mentally and emotionally. It was a huge undertaking that we were looking to take on, but it was one we needed to see through.

"He speaks very highly of the whole project. He wants to be involved and he keeps in contact with me. He's always asking if there is anything we need or if he could help us. I think he would like to take on an active role in the home."

"Good. That's good. I have spoken with Jay, and he is going to work with us on any paperwork we need. He also said if we register the group home as a non-profit, we would be able to apply for some Government funds. Grants. He said he would help out with all of the paperwork."

"That would be great. If we could have it registered, then we could really use those grants to help pay for any workers at the house. Dominic has a real estate buddy that he is going to introduce us to. He thinks we might be able to find an older hotel that we could renovate into a group home."

That would be ideal. We would need to renovate to accommodate for a rather large kitchen, but each kid would have their own room. They would also have their own bathroom. That would make things easier on us. We wouldn't have to worry about keeping the boys and girls separated or having two bathrooms both large enough to handle a good number of kids at one time.

Having their own bathroom would give them privacy that they all deserved. It would also give them a sense of responsibility. They would need to keep it clean, along with their room.

"We don't have an old hotel, though."

"We do have one, actually. It's older and abandoned, but it's on the South side of town, very close to the outskirts. It would need some serious work, but Dominic thinks the bones are good. It's just rundown and ugly. As long as the structure is good, it would be worth the investment to renovate."

"Okay, I'm good with renovating a current building. It would have to be cheaper than building one from the ground up. I've never noticed a hotel, but I don't tend to be on the South side of town often. That would be best for the kids. They could have their own space and privacy."

"I agree. I'll let Dominic know and we can set up a viewing. If you have Jay working on the paperwork to make it a legal non-profit, that will help us with some funding. Dr. Holland said he would volunteer as a therapist for the kids. We just need to find a couple more to volunteer to ease the pressure off of Dr. Holland."

"We also need to find a couple of people willing to work at the group home and live there. It would be best if we had a man and a woman so the boys and the girls will both feel comfortable."

"I agree, but that is going to take some time to find the right people. We'll have to do an extensive background check and make sure they are cleared to be responsible for that many children. What is our process going to be in choosing which children will be in the group home?"

That, I had no idea, because it wasn't as simple as putting kids that didn't have anywhere to go into the home. We had to make sure that the children were safe with the other children around. We had to make sure that any children who had serious psychological issues weren't a danger to any of the children or the caregiver. We needed to make sure we didn't turn our backs on a child that had issues, but we also had to make sure they weren't a threat to the home.

It would be a balancing act we would need to walk through, and I wasn't sure how to look at a child's file and decide if they were going to be placed in the home or not. If they didn't have anywhere to go, it was going to be very hard to turn them down. To place them somewhere else that might not be a permanent fit. I didn't want to have to say no to a child in need, but that was going to be a very real possibility.

Eventually, we would have all of the spaces filled and we would be right back to our current position. I wasn't sure what to do about that aspect of the whole process. We were always going to need more space, more room for the children, and we were always going to run out of that desperately needed space.

"I'm not sure what the process should be, yet. That's going to be the hardest part in all of this. We will need to have a set checklist for what children should be in the home and what ones we will need to find a more suitable place for. We will need to stick with it, no matter how hard it will be later on."

"It will be hard, but I agree we need to have a set process for our selection requirements. That is the only way we will be able to keep everything fair and keep everyone safe. As hard as it will be, I think it's for the best."

It would be hard. I didn't like having to turn children away, to tell them that they didn't qualify for a roof over their head. I knew we would be placing them in another foster home, though. It wasn't like we were just going to put them out on the street. Still, a foster home was a roll of the dice, even after all of the work we had done to correct the system. The system wasn't perfect and each kid we placed in a foster home was a coin flip and I hated that.

It was two hours later when we finally started to make progress on the long list of tasks we needed to plan and get organized. As we went through the process, the list of tasks that we needed to complete was getting longer and longer. I had no idea how we were ever going to be able to get it done, but I knew it would need to be completed before we could be open. Each task that got done, put us one step closer to having the group home open and that was all that mattered.

"This is going to take a long time to get done," Travis commented.

"We'll get it done, though. Do you have any plans for the weekend?"

I wanted to get to know more about him. I wanted him to know that he could tell me things and trust me with who he is. We had been working closely with each other for months now, and I wanted him to view me as a friend and not just a colleague.

"I'm just going to be finishing up painting. Yourself?"

"I have no plans. If you want, I could come by your place and help you finish painting," I offered.

"Oh, that's okay, I'll be fine. I only have one room left to get painted," Travis said, flashing me a warm smile.

"Well, if you change your mind, you

can always call me. Do you have any siblings in town?"

"No, I'm an only child."

"What about your parents?" I tried next.

"Both are dead. Why the interest all of a sudden?"

I could tell he was trying to not sound defensive, but I was able to pick it up just slightly. I knew he was a private person, but this seemed extreme to me.

We were colleagues, why wouldn't I want to know more about him?

It was a pretty common societal norm to want to know the people you worked with on a personal level, especially when you worked closely with them like we did. I was starting to get concerned that something was wrong for him to be so private.

"We've worked together for a good chunk of time, now, but I don't know anything about you or your life. You know quite a bit about me."

I said it casually, because I didn't want him to feel like I was attacking him. I didn't want him to pull away and be even more distant with me. When we first met, he barely spoke a single word to me unless he had to. Now, we were on a level where we could go for a meal or a cup of coffee together. It had taken a long time to get to this point. I didn't want to lose it and have to start at square one again.

"There's not much to tell, really. I work and then I go home and do more work. I don't have much of a social life. There's not really anything to talk about."

I highly doubted that. He could have very easily been an indoor cat, but I suspected he was hiding something. I wished I knew how to get him to open up to me. How to get him to share some of his personal life with me.

There were plenty of times where he looked stressed and rundown. I had always asked how he was doing, but he blew it off as a late night watching movies instead of sleeping. I always let it go, because it wasn't my place to try and force something out of him, but I was getting more worried about him as time went on. Something was going on with him and I had no idea what it could be.

I was afraid that he might be sick. That maybe, he didn't want anyone to know about it. Or perhaps, his place was a complete disaster. He wouldn't be the first person to have a hoarding issue and still be able to hold down a job. This job took a lot out on a person, so it wouldn't be that surprising if he had issues within his personal life.

Whatever was going on with Travis, I would find out. I was not about to allow him to face this world on his own, even if he believed he had to. I was going to be there for him and, hopefully, with time he would feel more comfortable opening up to me and sharing more personal details about himself and his life. We were in this together and I was not about to let him feel otherwise.

# CHAPTER TWENTY-SIX

Sol

"THAT PLACE SEEMED nice," I said as Isaiah and I strolled down the street.

It had been three months since we started to date each other, and the past three months had been amazing. I couldn't have ever imagined that I could be so happy.

That someone could make me this

happy.

I kept waiting for when I would wake up and discover the past three months had all been a dream.

A wonderful dream.

So far, I hadn't woken up, thank God.

I never wanted this dream to end.

Over the past three months, we had taken things slow. We had yet to have sex, but the sexual tension between us was building and soon it was going to explode.

I wanted it to explode so freaking badly.

After the past three months, I had more than enough saved up for an apartment and I had just been waiting for the opportunity for one to come up. This apartment had gone up on the market yesterday and I jumped on it. It was a two bedroom and was located within the downtown area, so it would still be close to River's school and my work.

Isaiah had offered to come with me. He gave me a ride so I wouldn't have to worry about trying to get back to work without being late. He had even been teaching me how to drive so I would be able to take on construction jobs outside of town. I didn't know if I would like to drive, but I found it relaxing and Isaiah was a great teacher, in and out of the bedroom.

"It was, yeah. There is another option, though," Isaiah said as he stopped and moved in front of me so we were facing each other.

"And what would that be?"

"Move in with me. I have two spare bedrooms. We don't have to share a room until you're ready. But move in with me."

Now that was the best offer I had ever heard in my life. I knew it would be crazy. I knew, logically, I shouldn't be moving in with him. We had only started dating three months prior, but screw logic.

I had been operating for so long on making sure River and I were safe. I had been relying on my instincts and logical side to keep us alive. It was time I made a decision based on my own emotions, my own desires. And I knew River would love it. He liked Isaiah and he liked being there.

"Hell yes, but on one condition."

"Name it," Isaiah easily agreed.

"We keep a spare bedroom," I said with a flirty smirk, and Isaiah knew exactly what I meant.

There was no way I was going to be living with this man and not sleeping in his bed every night. I wanted to fall asleep in his arms and wake up in them. I didn't want to miss a single second with him.

"You drive a hard bargain, but I accept your conditions," Isaiah said with a playful smile.

I loved this man.

I was madly in love with him and I never wanted this to end. I never wanted to miss a single second with him, a single moment. It was time I took full control of my life, to embrace living. I ran my hand down his chest as I spoke.

"I think I'm starting to come down with something."

Isaiah flashed me a warm smile and a wink. He clearly understood what I was getting at. I had never skipped work before. I would normally never even think about skipping it. Even when I was very sick, I would still show up to make money, but I didn't have to do that right now.

I had money saved up.

I was making very good money.

I could afford to skip one day.

"Now that you mention it, my head does hurt," Isaiah said, a smile splitting his face.

"We should probably lay down. It would be the responsible thing to do."

"I agree." Isaiah took my hand and we quickly made our way to his car. I didn't know if we would finally have sex, but I was really hoping that was what would happen once we got back to his place. Well, *our place*, technically.

# EPILOGUE

Sol

HIS LIPS AND hands were all over me the second we walked through the front door. Our need was way too strong, and I doubted either one of us were going to be able to hold out for very long.

I removed his suit jacket as I kicked off my boots.

"I want you," I said, my mouth

hovering against his lips as we took a moment to catch our breath.

"God, yes," Isaiah moaned out as he pulled me toward him and started to guide us to the stairs.

We continued to remove the other's clothing as we made our way to the bedroom. By the time we reached the bedroom, we were both naked and hard.

Isaiah kicked the door closed as he backed me up to the bed. I collapsed down onto it and pulled Isaiah with me. I easily opened my legs and allowed him to slide between them.

The second our hard dicks touched each other we were both moaning deeply. I didn't think I would ever get tired of this. The way Isaiah could make me feel was unbelievable and I never wanted it to end.

"I need to feel you inside me."

Isaiah started to kiss all along my neck as I spoke. He pulled back and looked down at me. I could see the heat in his eyes, but I could also tell he was going to be serious now.

"Are you sure? There's no rush, Honey."

"I have never been more sure of anything in my life. If you are ready, I'm ready."

I didn't want to rush him, but I was really hoping he wanted to have sex right now. I was dying to feel him inside of me and I was hoping he felt the same way.

"I am more than ready, Honey." Isaiah reached over to his bedside table and pulled out some lube. He flashed me a smirk as he spoke.

I grabbed him by the back of his neck and pulled him down to me. Instantly, his mouth was devouring mine. I ran my hands down his back until I grabbed his ass and pulled his hips against mine, causing us both to moan.

Isaiah kissed his way down my neck and then my abs as I vaguely heard the lid of the lube to snap open. We had done all of this before, including him finger fucking me, but we never went further than that.

Today, we were finally going to go all the way and I couldn't wait.

A moan escaped me as Isaiah hovered over the head of my cock, his hot breath making me even harder. I arched my back as he gave my dick a long lick before he took me into his mouth all the way.

The man was beyond gifted in the sex department. I didn't have much to compare him to, at least none that I wanted to remember, but it didn't matter. I knew he was talented and no man would ever be able to make me feel like this again.

I felt Isaiah insert his finger into me and I opened my legs more to give him better access. It didn't take long before I was writhing with need on the bed. He always knew how to work my body to bring me the greatest pleasure.

Once I was stretched enough, Isaiah removed his fingers from my ass and, much to my displeasure, pulled his mouth off my dick with an audible pop.

"I want to be inside of you when you come." He kissed my hip, nibbling as he spoke.

"Yes, please."

Isaiah kissed and nibbled his way up my body as he added more lube to his dick. When he reached my neck, I felt the tip of his hardness against my hole. I moaned at just the feel of it outside of me. I wanted it inside of me so fucking badly.

"You sure?" Isaiah asked once again.

"If you don't put it inside of me, I will."

Isaiah gave a soft chuckle before he spoke.

"Next time you can ride me all night long, Honey."

A shiver ran down my entire body at that promise. It was one I was planning on cashing in on.

Isaiah placed his hand underneath my thigh and lifted my hips slightly to give him better access and a better angle. He then slowly started to push inside of me and I let out a throaty moan as I felt his tip breach my hole. He already felt amazing and it was only his tip.

Isaiah let out a groan and I knew he would be feeling extraordinary right at this moment. He had never done this before, so he had no idea how tight and warm it would be inside of me.

Bit by bit, he pushed in until his large length and thickness was completely inside of me. He stopped once he was balls deep and placed his forehead against mine as he breathed heavily, allowing me to accommodate to his invasion.

"You're so tight and hot."

"You are so big. You feel so good. So good, Baby. I'm ready. Move when you're ready."

"It's going to be quick."

"Good. Make it hard and fast. We can do slow after."

There was nothing that I wanted more

than to feel him lose control inside of me.

I wanted to feel his passion.

I wanted to feel him come deep inside of me.

That was all he needed to hear before he pulled out almost all of the way and immediately he pushed right back in. He did a few slower thrusts before he started to pound me with everything he had in him, and it was glorious.

I wrapped my legs around his hips and pushed my hips up to meet his thrusts. The new position made him go even deeper inside of me, and when his dick hit my sweet spot dead on, I couldn't contain the scream of pleasure that escaped my lips.

"Fuck. Baby, don't stop," I moaned, arching my back and snapping my hips upward to meet him.

"You feel so good. So freaking good, Honey. I could do this all day and night long and never be tired of how amazing you feel," he said as he picked up the pace even more.

His thrusts started to become erratic and I knew he was reaching his edge. I was already seconds away from falling off that cliff and when he hit my sweet spot again. I wasn't just tumbling off, I was free falling and I was never going to stop.

"Isaiah!" I screamed as I pulsed long and hard. Shooting an endless amount of cum between our bodies.

The tightness of my walls around his dick was enough to push Isaiah right over the edge with me. I had no idea how amazing it would feel to have him coming inside of me, but the combination of his pulsing dick and his hot cum, it made me see stars and come even more.

The room was filled with our groans and heavy breathing as we both lost the fight to the pleasure that overtook us. I was seeing stars and my legs were tingling. Hell, my whole body was euphoric and buzzing.

It wasn't just sex, it was earth shattering, ruining me for other men sex, and I loved every single second of it.

Isaiah had been able to come back down to Earth faster than me. He placed a few gentle and soft kisses to my lips as he tried to get his breathing back under control.

"You're remarkable," he said softly in between peppering kisses over my face and lips.

"So are you. I love you."

It came out before my mind was even

able to register the words. I probably shouldn't have said it. It was too early in our relationship to be at the love stage. At least, I thought it was. Now, there was a good chance I was going to ruin our relationship.

"I love you, too," Isaiah said, a deep emotion filling his voice.

It was that tone, and the look of pure devotion and love in his eyes that told me he meant it.

He meant every single word.

He wasn't just saying it back to avoid an awkward moment.

This man truly did love me.

I had somehow managed to have a great man like Isaiah fall in love with me.

When I was a kid, I believed in fairy tales. I used to dream about a prince coming to save me. He would show up on his horse in a suit of armor and he would take me away to his kingdom.

As I got older, I knew there was no such thing as princes. And certainly no one was going to be coming to save me. But in this moment, I knew without a doubt or an ounce of uncertainty that I was wrong.

Fairy tales did exist, because my prince had shown up. He wasn't in a suit of armor or riding a horse, but he was real. And now, I was never going to let him go.

Thank you for reading!

***

Tormented is the final book in the From The Edge series...for now.

I know, it's going to be very difficult to

say goodbye to some of these characters, BUT if you would like to continue reading delicious man love tales, you can pickup the first book in my new series, Federal Protection Agency. There, I am sure you will find some old friends and new ones as you traverse Mason's world. I'll warn you now, there may be a lot of triggers in the new series as the FPA men fight to bring to justice the evil that perpetuates crimes against children, but I am sure it'll be worth it.

For a taste of book one, Mason, all you have to do is turn the page…

Watch for Mason, Federal Protection Agency, book one, at your favorite online retailer!

# PREVIEW

Mason

*POSTTRAUMATIC STRESS DISORDER is a psychiatric disorder that may occur in people who have experienced or witnessed a traumatic event such as a natural disaster, a serious accident, a terrorist act, war/combat, or rape, or who have been threatened with death, sexual violence, or serious injury. Symptoms include: intrusive thoughts, nightmares, avoiding reminders of the event, memory loss, negative thoughts about self and the world, self-isolation, feeling distant, anger and irritability, reduced interest in favorite activities, hyper vigilance, difficulty concentrating, insomnia, vivid flashbacks, avoiding people, places and things related to the event, casting blame, difficulty feeling positive emotions, exaggerated startle response, and risky behaviors.*

"What a bunch of bullshit," I said, and tossed my phone onto the dash of my rental truck.

The shrink I had hired to help me with my insomnia had just diagnosed me with PTSD and it was a load of shit. Just because I had some of the symptoms, didn't mean that was what was wrong with me.

I was able to function.

I was doing my job.

I just had some problems outside of it.

I was having a hard time sleeping, and when I did, I usually had nightmares. I was a bit on edge, but never in the field. I wasn't angry or lashing out at people. I wasn't having flashbacks or panic attacks. Sure, at times, I had a hard time sitting still. I got anxious sometimes at night but I would just go for a run with Koda and I was fine.

I didn't have PTSD.

Besides, I didn't even know where it would have come from. I was a federal agent with Homeland security. I specialized in crimes against children and, yes, I saw some horrific things, but nothing that the other Agents hadn't already seen.

Agents that had been on the job for twenty years were fine with the things we see, so how could that give me PTSD when it didn't with others?

The shrink was wrong. It was just that simple. Everyone struggled with sleeping from time to time.

And if I had to have a few drinks in the day to get through the night, then so what?

I never drank while on duty. It was always after work. I wasn't drinking an excessive amount, just enough to help me fall asleep when it had been a few days. I was coping and there was nothing wrong with it.

Koda whined beside me and I glanced over at him. Koda was my K9 partner, a beautiful German shepherd.

I loved this dog.

I didn't know what I would do without him.

I've always loved dogs and when the opportunity presented itself for me to be a K9 handler five years ago, I jumped at the chance. I've had Koda ever since he was an eight week old puppy, and I couldn't imagine not having him in my life.

My greatest fear is for Koda to be hurt in the field.

"You want to go and see Uncle Ro?" I asked the dog as I started to pet him. I was currently sitting in my rental truck out front of my older brother's house.

Roland, or Ro as I always called him, was a local cop. He was also ex-military and had been a cop in New York City before he moved out here. I was surprised when he decided to move to a smaller town like Gaithersburg, but it was his life and he was free to do with it as he wished.

He knew I was coming by, that I had taken some vacation days. He didn't know about the real troubles I'd been having with my sleep. I wasn't about to tell him and add to his own worries and stress.

Letting out yet another sigh, I removed my seatbelt and got out. I might as well get this over and done with. The second we opened the door and strolled inside, Koda ran right toward the kitchen where I knew Roland would be.

"Hello, my sweet boy," Roland said as he started to pet Koda. "You know he loves me better, right?" he teased as he looked right at me.

I couldn't help but roll my eyes.

"He only likes you because you slip him food from the table when you think

I'm not looking."

Roland was terrible at keeping Koda on his proper diet and schedule. He was always slipping him people food, even when he knew he wasn't supposed to be. It wasn't that Koda couldn't have a treat, but he had to earn it. He needed to work for it. That wasn't my rule, it was the rule for all of the working dogs.

"How was the trip?" Roland asked as he reluctantly moved away from Koda and opened his arms to give me a hug.

Roland was massive. It never failed to gain attention. He was twice my size and I wasn't a small guy. I had muscles and was more than capable of holding my own in a fight.

Roland had taught me how to fight. When I decided I wanted to be a federal agent, Roland had made sure I would be able to handle anything that came my way. He trained me in multiple fighting styles and shooting. He made sure I was ready for any fight.

We had a similar look, though, in terms of hair, eye color, and the shape of our face. You could tell by looking at us that we were brothers. We were both good looking and both gay. Though, unlike me, Roland took a long time to come out.

"Not bad. Airplanes are nothing for me. So what's been going on since we've last spoken? You seem to be in a better mood than you were a few days ago. I expected to find you on the couch in sweatpants with empty pizza boxes and beer cans all around you."

When we had last spoken, Roland was in a dark place. The guy that he liked, Tyler, hadn't spoken to him in a couple of weeks. He had also taken a week off of work.

It was the first time he had truly liked another guy since he had lost Shane. Shane was the man that he was madly in love with when he was younger and still in the Army.

Shane was out and proud, but Roland had been afraid to come out. Don't Ask, Don't Tell, was no longer in effect, but that didn't mean an organization flooded with alpha males would be open minded about serving next to a gay man.

Roland had stayed in the closet and there was only so long Shane could handle it. One night, after an epic fight, Shane stormed off in the car, only to be hit by a drunk driver. Shane died on impact and the drunk driver got away. Roland then quit the Army and joined the

NYPD. He was the one that caught his lover's killer a few years later. Roland hadn't been in a relationship with anyone since.

"Tyler came over last night. We had a great conversation," he said, and flashed a warm smile.

"Oh, just a conversation?" I teased as I grabbed some coffee and headed for the table.

"A bit more than that. It started off with a conversation. He told me that he needed time to get his feelings in order and to process everything that had just happened."

"Makes sense, he thought he was straight his whole life. Having a guy kiss you out of nowhere can be shocking," I said with complete understanding to my voice.

"And that was my fault for doing it that way. It came out of nowhere. Thankfully, though, I didn't scare him off for very long. He told me he had feelings for me, too. That he didn't even sleep with the two women he had been dating in the past two months. He's actually never slept with a woman before, or anyone."

"Damn, you bagged yourself a twenty-two year old virgin. Now I'm jealous."

I was a sucker for a virgin or a spinner. I liked the smaller guys, the ones that you could toss around and overpower. I wasn't a fan of vanilla sex. I liked to have power over my lover. I liked to use toys and restraints. Sex was supposed to be fun and I believed in trying many different flavors of it. I tended to go for smaller guys, because they loved to bottom and I was only a top.

"The point is, we are taking things slow. We watched a movie and made out a bit last night before we went to sleep, in separate rooms. I'm trying to make him feel comfortable and allow him to stay in control of the sexual progress."

"I am happy for you. It's been a very long time since you've allowed yourself to be with another man. I know what happened with Shane was devastating, but you've kinda been putting your whole life on pause, Ro. I don't know what it's like to lose the man you love, and I didn't know him as well as I should have, but he wouldn't want this for you. He wouldn't want you to be alone and heartbroken for the rest of your life."

"I'm trying. What about you? Any new guy in your life?"

"Not right now, no. I've been too busy

with work. I'm not really the dating type, anyway. It's easier to keep things to friends with benefits or one-night stands."

I held zero interest in dating someone. With my job, it really wasn't even possible. I worked too many hours and I traveled all over the country at a moment's notice. It wasn't conducive to a healthy relationship.

"Always such a romantic," Roland teased, and once again I rolled my eyes.

Before I could comment, Koda's head snapped up and looked right at the door. Instantly, I was on edge and ready for an attack. I knew it wasn't a normal reaction, but it was what always happened, now, when there was a knock at the door or the phone rang. I was always ready for an ambush and there was nothing I could do about it.

"You expecting someone?" I asked, doing my best to keep my voice calm and casual. I wasn't sure if I was able to pull it off.

"It's Isaiah, my friend with Social Services. He's coming by so we can talk about the foster home situation," Roland answered as he got up to let him in.

Roland had told me about Tyler, his current love interest, and his old partner, Jasper Monroe's reaction to each other. When he told me that Tyler seemed scared of his old foster father, I could tell it was bothering him.

Tyler had grown up in the foster care system and, for a couple of years, he'd had Monroe as his foster father. Monroe had never told Roland about it, not even after him and Tyler started to hang out. We both found their reactions to each other suspicious and decided that it should be looked into.

It wasn't common for a former foster child to have that much fear toward a foster father. Something had to have happened and I was worried what it was. I didn't want my brother to be caught in a deadly situation if it came back that Monroe was a dirty cop.

"Hey man, come on in," Roland said warmly as he opened the door.

I peaked around the corner so I could see what Isaiah looked like. I don't know what I was expecting for Isaiah, but I wasn't expecting what stood on the other side of the door. The man was a bit chubby and average looking, probably a teddy bear, but he looked like a wreck. Like he hadn't slept in days. I wasn't sure, but something was going on with him.

"Is your brother here?" he asked as he walked in.

"Yeah, in the kitchen. Come on back and grab a coffee. You look like you could use it."

"You wouldn't believe what I found, Roland," he said as they ambled toward the kitchen.

I had no idea what he had found, but by how he was behaving, he found something huge.

My gut said it was something I wasn't going to like.

"Mason, this is Isaiah. He works with Social Services and is who I reached out to about intel on Tyler," Roland said to me.

"It's nice to meet you," I said as I held my hand out for Isaiah to take.

He easily clasped my hand in his

before he spoke.

"Nice to meet you. I have a feeling we're going to need your help on this one."

I didn't like the sound of that. It was one thing to need a cop, but to need a federal agent, that meant something huge had happened.

"What did you find?" Roland asked, getting things started.

"I started by looking through Tyler's time with Jasper. As you know, he was there between the ages of twelve and fourteen. He was one of eight foster kids, sometimes a little less over the two years. On the surface, it all seems perfectly normal and there weren't any red flags in Tyler's file for Jasper. Before that, he had been through a lot of rough homes and had been abused. It all stopped for two years before he was sent to another foster home, and then it picked up all over again."

"Okay, but I'm not hearing anything to imply that something is wrong with Jasper. Sounds like you need to review all of the foster homes in the system, though," I said.

It wasn't uncommon for there to be a few bad apples within the foster home system. However, it sounded like they had more than a couple in this town.

"Tyler was diagnosed with a protein deficiency when he was eight. It makes it hard for him to gain weight. Aside from that, and the asthma, he was perfectly healthy. Broken bones and bruising, but no illnesses. For the two years he was with Jasper, everything was perfect. Too perfect. Bruises were gone, he went to school, everything was normal and without complaint. Then, all of a sudden, he is being transferred, by Jasper's request to another home and the hell started all over again. Only, he was there for two days when he started to get very sick. His social worker saw how sick he was and took him to the hospital. They ran his bloodwork and discovered he was going through cocaine withdrawal."

"Whoa, what?" Roland asked, shocked and outraged.

That wasn't good.

That confirmed that something more was going on within that foster home and it wasn't going to end well.

"There was no way of telling how it got into his system, just that it was there. His social worker asked where he got the drugs, but he clammed up. Jasper was brought in to be questioned, but he was a Detective, even back then, so the worker believed everything he said. He said Tyler must have gotten it from school, that he had no idea. They went with Jasper's story and never looked into his home or any of the other children."

"It's not uncommon for children in their young teenage years to get their hands on cocaine. I find it hard to believe that no one would have noticed. If he was going through physical withdrawals, he had to have been doing it for months and in large doses. Were any of the other children checked out?" I asked.

"That's the thing, the social worker never spoke to any of the current children or looked through his home. So, I did." He placed a rather large brown file on the table as he continued. "That is Jasper's and his wife, Dana's, fostering file. It includes every child they have ever taken in, including the current ones. Currently, he has nine kids all between the ages of nine and fourteen. I've started to go through the process of pulling the previous foster children's files, but there are over a hundred and fifty of them."

"Shit," Roland said, obviously shocked that it was that many.

That *was* a fast turnaround.

I knew that some homes kids came and went at one hell of a pace, however, that was usually in larger cities. The smaller cities, the kids tended to stay with their one foster parent unless something was wrong with them. Kids didn't tend to get passed around like Christmas candy in towns this size, as a general rule. There was no reason for Monroe to have that many previous children.

I was getting a bad feeling about this and it wasn't going to end well. Monroe was Roland's past partner. They were still partners when they needed backup on a case. This wasn't going to go well if Monroe was dirty, and it was starting to look like he was.

"It's going to take some time to pull all of their files and go through them to see if any doctor reports were made after their time with Jasper. Some were also moved to another city and I don't have access to their files," Isaiah continued.

"I can get 'em. I just need their names and I can pull the file, no matter where they were placed in the country. We need to do a sneak and peek at Monroe's house and see what is going on. I'm assuming you are operating under the impression that Monroe is cooking drugs in the house," I stated.

I had come here for a vacation, but I also knew that Roland was worried about Tyler. It was the least I could do after everything my brother had done for me.

"Last night, I looked through twenty files. Twelve of the kids were admitted to the hospital with withdrawal-like symptoms. Not all of them were given blood work. Most were told it was the flu and they would feel better in a few days. It's enough for me to make the hypothesis that cocaine is being either cooked at the house around the children, or the children were weighing and packaging the cocaine."

"That sounds like a reasonable hypothesis. I've never noticed any problems with Jasper being sick, though, in three years," Roland stated.

"Depends. I've gone into a lot of homes where the drugs were made in the basement and the kids were sick but the foster parents weren't. The kids were the ones touching the drugs and breathing it in as they were either cooking or packaging it. The parents were fine, because the ventilation system in the upstairs of the house was solid. It kept the fumes down in the basement and when they needed to go down there, they wore the proper protection. It's completely logical that Monroe isn't breathing it in. Just like it's logical that he is breathing it in, but he's never not been around it. His body could be addicted to it and he gets his fix by being in the house," I pointed out.

"Let's get the files and go through

them. See which kids were hospitalized after leaving Jasper's. I'll loop in Captain Perry so he's aware of the situation. Yes, we'll need to do a sneak and peek at his house. Mase, can you get a warrant from a judge? We gotta keep that out of town."

"I'll get it. With those files, we should have enough for a warrant," I said confidently. That was easy enough to do and I agreed that it needed to be out of town. A town this size, everyone knew everyone and no judge was going to give us a sneak and peek warrant with what we had.

"Okay, I have to go to the office and start pulling them. Do you want to join me there, or do you want me to bring them back here?" Isaiah asked.

"It would be better to do it here. We don't know who will talk to who. I want to try and keep this as quiet as possible," Roland answered.

"I'll be back in about an hour or so, then," Isaiah said, before he finished his coffee and headed out.

"I'll grab my bag and get my laptop out of it. I'll get A.S.A Crawford up to speed and he'll grab us a warrant," I said as I stood.

"Not exactly the vacation you were looking for. I'm sorry."

"It's okay. The drug cases are the easiest. Have you thought about just asking Tyler again? Tell him you know that Jasper could be mixed up with drugs."

It would make things easier if he talked to Tyler about it. It was most likely the reason why Tyler didn't want to talk about Monroe. That old fear was still inside of him, but if Roland could get him to open up, it would help a lot.

I might not be able to get a sneak and peek warrant with what we had. We might need Tyler to go on the record about what happened in that house to do something about it.

"No, I want to keep him out of this. I don't know what is going on, but I know that when drug dealers feel threatened, they'll attack the one they feel is responsible. I don't want Tyler getting hurt. It's better to leave him in the dark."

"It's your call. I'll support you in whatever you decide, Ro. I'll go grab my gear," I said with complete understanding to my voice.

I knew how dangerous drug dealers could be, especially with children. If he didn't want to bring Tyler into this just yet, that was his call and I would respect it.

Hopefully, we wouldn't need Tyler and I could secure us a warrant without anyone on record.

One thing was for certain, this wasn't the type of vacation I had been planning.

Snag your copy of Mason now at your favorite online retailer!

# OTHER BOOKS BY EVIE

**Federal Protection Agency**

Mason

Rafe

Ryzen

Cooper

Noah

Damien

Sebastian

Gabe

Logan

**Ruthless Empire**

Courting Danger

Chasing Danger

Kissing Danger

**Smokejumpers**

Hawke

Cyrus

Jase

Gage

Jackson

Xavier

**Jasper Springs**
Cade
Dawson
Drew
Grayson
Riley
Mitch


**From The Edge**
Shattered
Runaway
Jaded
Rescue
Hidden
Tormented


**Gray Vale Pack**
His Fated Mate
His Wounded Warrior
His Healing Heart

# ABOUT THE AUTHOR

Evie Riley is a prolific, neurodivergent author known for her captivating MM romance novels. She has gained a significant following and topped the LGBT+ action and adventure bestseller charts with her series.

Evie's writing style often explores dark and gritty themes where her men must overcome difficult obstacles in their search for love, but she has also ventured into sweeter small-town romances, incorporating tropes like enemies-to-lovers, friends-to-lovers, age-gap, and forced proximity. She is known for crafting engaging romantic suspense novels and has a knack for creating interconnected series worlds that keep readers invested.

Interestingly, Ms. Riley has hinted at exploring new genres, such as Alien Omegaverse Romance, in the future.

Outside of writing, she enjoys spending time at the beach and has a quirky personality, described by her partner as ranging from cute to deadly, depending on her blood-chocolate levels.

Evie spends her nights writing bad boys in love, and her days wrangling the sweet boys she loves.